EMILY DAVIS

Also by Miss Read

VILLAGE SCHOOL
VILLAGE DIARY
STORM IN THE VILLAGE
THRUSH GREEN
FRESH FROM THE COUNTRY
WINTER IN THRUSH GREEN
MISS CLARE REMEMBERS
OVER THE GATE
VILLAGE CHRISTMAS
THE MARKET SQUARE
THE HOWARDS OF CAXLEY
THE FAIRACRE FESTIVAL

EMILY DAVIS

by Miss Read

Illustrated by J. S. Goodall

Houghton Mifflin Company, Boston

1972

First Printing C

First American Edition 1972

ISBN: 0-395-13524-9
Library of Congress Catalog Card Number: 73-177543
Printed in the United States of America

To
Beryl and Philip
with love

And some there be, which have no memorial; who are perished, as though they had never been . . .

But these were merciful men, whose righteousness hath not been forgotten . . .

The people will tell of their wisdom, and the congregation will show forth their praise.

Ecclesiasticus, Chapter 44

CONTENTS

1 Two Old Friends

ONE golden September evening, Dolly Clare and her friend Emily Davis set out on a walk at the edge of Hundred Acre Field, which lay behind the hawthorn hedge of their cottage home.

It was a leisurely progress; more of a potter than a true walk. There were frequent stops to admire the scarlet rose-hips in the hedge, or to pick a spray of late honeysuckle, or simply to stand, eyes shaded against the declining sun's dazzle, to gaze across the great field to the hazy blue of the downs beyond.

But then both ladies were in their eighties, slight and silver-haired, and the track was rough going even for the young and sure-footed.

Besides, why hurry? Their time, after years of teaching in the village schools near Caxley, was their own, and had been ever since retirement some twenty years earlier. Their days were as serene and cloudless as the evening air which they were now enjoying. The clock, once their stern task-master, had no power over them now.

The two had met at Beech Green village school when Emily Davis was seven, and Dolly Clare, then a timid newcomer, was six years old.

'You can sit by Emily,' the teacher had said to the bewildered Dolly. 'Emily Davis will look after you.'

The dark little girl had shifted along the desk seat obligingly,

and given Dolly a wide smile, made more endearing by the gap left by the loss of her two front teeth.

From that moment they had been friends, and Dolly grew to love Emily even more deeply than she did her own older sister Ada.

The little house which Emily shared with her six brothers and sisters became a second home to young Dolly. Somehow, there was always room for one more child to tumble about in the crowded living room at the Davis' cottage.

The two little girls had shared their schooling at Beech Green School and later had travelled almost three miles together each morning to attend Fairacre School in the next village.

They knew every foot of the road intimately. They knew where a robin had his nest, where white violets were hidden, where there were blackberries to quench a child's thirst and the first primroses to carry proudly home. Their love of nature's treasures was doubly deep because it was shared. It was to be a never-failing source of happiness to them throughout their lives.

They both became pupil teachers, attending evening classes at Caxley, the local market town, and trying out their skills with the younger children at Fairacre.

Their ways later divided, but were never far apart, and weekly letters held the bond between the two friends. The Great War of 1914–1918 brought tragedy to them both. Dolly Clare's fiancé, Arnold Fletcher, was killed at Ypres, and Emily had, perhaps, an even harder blow to bear. Edgar, whom she loved dearly, lay ill in a war-time hospital for many months. Week after week, Emily made the difficult journey to see him, sustained by the hope of his progress to health and their future happiness.

It was a bitter day for Emily when she received a letter from him confessing that he had fallen in love with his nurse, and all was over.

Later, he brought his wife to live near Fairacre, and it was Emily's painful lot to witness the progress of the marriage.

She was careful to keep out of the way of Edgar and his family, but she heard from many neighbours that the marriage was an unhappy one. The nurse had proved a nagger, and Edgar, once so gay, had become sullen with the years. The knowledge distressed Emily, but she said nothing.

The two friends never married. There were very few eligible men left in their generation, and they filled their days busily with work for other people's children. When the time came to retire, Dolly Clare left Fairacre School, and continued to live in the same little cottage, thatched by her father Francis Clare, at the foot of the downs.

A few years later, Emily came to join her, and a period of perfect companionship began for the old friends. Their ways fell together as sweetly as the two halves of an apple, and every day held simple joys.

This evening walk was one of them. They had walked this track watching the corn sprout, grow, turn from green to gold, and had listened to the clamour of the combine harvester as it gathered the grain. The baler had been at work during the past few days, and neatly-stacked piles, seven bales to each, stood among the glistening stubble awaiting collection.

Overhead the rooks flapped slowly homeward uttering their raucous cries, and, in the distance, pin-points of flame on the hill side showed where a farmer was burning his stubble, with thoughts of ploughing to come already in his mind.

The pair walked to the oak tree which stood in the hedge. Soon the acorns would be ripe enough to fall.

'We shall soon see the pheasants gathering round here,' observed Dolly.

'I've always loved the autumn,' said Emily. They stood in the oak tree's shade, gazing up into its gnarled branches.

Emily shivered, and Dolly noticed it.

'It's chilly here,' she said. 'Let's go home. There begins to get a nip in the air when the sun goes down.'

They turned to face the silvered thatch above the hawthorn hedge and, like the rooks above them, made their way home.

The evening was spent sitting one each side of the fireplace. Dolly had put a match to the paper and sticks which always stood ready in the hearth, and a small fire of logs now crackled cheerfully.

'It seems extravagant,' said Emily, lowering her knitting and gazing at the flames. 'And only September! But what a joy a fire is, Dolly, isn't it? Thank goodness, we've still the strength to bring in a bit of firing.'

They listened to a little music on their ancient radio set, knitting the while, and basking in the warmth from the fire.

At eight o'clock Dolly fetched supper on a tray for them both. Thin brown bread and butter, a little cottage cheese, and two bowls of blackberries, dappled with the cream from the top of the milk, made their meal, with a glass of warm milk apiece to wash it down.

'We're like the good rabbits, Flopsy, Mopsy and Cotton-tail,' commented Emily, laughing, 'with our "bread and milk and blackberries for supper".'

'I wonder how many hundreds of times we've read that,' said Dolly.

'Recited it,' corrected Emily. 'We certainly never needed to look at the pages.'

They fell to reminiscing, as they did so often, while the meal was in progress. Their memories were prodigious, and their enjoyment of the follies and foibles of their neighbours, past and present, was as keen as ever.

The meal over, they washed up together in the little kitchen. Emily gave a great yawn.

'I can't think why I'm so sleepy tonight. I feel just as I did after a ten-mile walk as a girl. A lovely feeling really – but just dog-tired.'

'Go up to bed early,' urged Dolly. 'Shall I help you up-stairs?'

'No, no!' cried Emily robustly. 'There's nothing wrong with me. But I think I will go up, as you say.'

She took her book and made her way up the short staircase. Dolly, below, heard the creaking of the old floorboards as she made ready for bed, and the gentle squeak of the springs as Emily settled herself.

Dolly knitted for a little longer. The logs were almost burned through, black and zebra-striped with silvery ash. The cat had taken advantage of Emily's absence to establish itself in her chair. There, curled up luxuriously, it would stay until morning, unless the mysterious noises of the night tempted it through the window left ajar for its convenience.

The sky was clear when Miss Clare made her way to bed at ten o'clock. A great full moon silvered the sleeping world. From her bedroom window Dolly noted the luminous beauty of the field of stubble, beside which she had walked with Emily a few hours earlier. She was reminded of Samuel Palmer's pictures of the countryside. He had caught exactly that eerie moonlight transfiguring an everyday world.

In the distance a sheep coughed, rasping and rhythmic, like an asthmatic old man.

It was very still. The perfume of night-scented stock came from the garden bed beneath the window. Emily, who loved the scent, had planted the seeds that spring.

Reminded of her by the fragrance of the flowers, Dolly went softly across the landing.

Emily had put out her light, but lay awake, gazing at the bands of moonlight across the rafters.

'All right, my dear?' asked Dolly gently.

'Perfectly,' answered Emily. 'What a heavenly night!'

'Can I bring you anything?'

'Nothing, dear, thank you. I've all I want.'

'Then sleep well,' said Dolly.

She kissed her friend's forehead briefly, and closing the door behind her made her way to her own room.

She was asleep within twenty minutes, but Emily, next door, was not. Tired though she was, sleep seemed to evade her.

She plumped up her pillows and sat up in bed. Now she could see the tops of the trees in the garden, the cornfield and the distant downs. Somewhere at hand a night bird rustled among leaves, and in the thatch above her there was a tiny scratching noise. No doubt a mouse was out upon its foragings.

The peace of the countryside enveloped her. Had it ever been so beautiful? Lit by the full moon, scented with stocks, the familiar view was enhanced by the mystery of night.

Emily sat there entranced for almost an hour. She had known that scene for eighty years, and still it had power to move and delight her, to present a different aspect with every changing season, and with every changing hour.

At last, with a sigh of pleasure, she sank back upon her pillows and closed her eyes.

2 Dolly Clare Alone

MISS Clare woke early. The hands of the china clock pointed to six o'clock, as she sat up in bed to survey the day.

The sun was slowly dispersing the light mist which veiled the distant downs. The beech hedge was draped with filmy cobwebs, and the grass was grey with a heavy autumn dew.

'There should be mushrooms about,' said Miss Clare aloud.

The shadow of the cottage, elongated absurdly, stretched across the cornfield. The chimneys were just like rabbits' ears, thought Dolly Clare, with amusement.

The croaking cry of a pheasant came from the distance. No doubt he was searching for a few early acorns from the oak tree. There had been another picking of ripe blackberries close to the tree, Dolly remembered. She would take her basket there later in the morning when the sun had dried the long grass a little. Emily enjoyed a dish of blackberry and apple meringue, and there were plenty of apples and eggs in the larder.

She wondered if Emily were awake, but decided not to disturb her so early. Countrywomen both, they were usually astir by seven o'clock, but Emily had seemed so tired, it would be a good thing if she slept on, thought Dolly.

She rose, and dressed as quietly as possible, but no matter how lightly she trod, the ancient floor boards creaked and squeaked, and the staircase was equally noisy as she crept downstairs.

She opened the windows and doors, letting in the fresh morning air scented still with stocks and damp grass. It was Dolly's favourite time of day, when the world was cool and quiet, and the day was full of hope.

She fed the purring cat which rubbed about her legs, and then set the breakfast table. Next she filled the kettle and switched it on. To have an electric kettle which boiled within five minutes, was still a wonder to Dolly Clare, who well remembered the lengthy process of lighting the kitchen fire and waiting for the black iron kettle to boil above it.

She thought she heard a sound above. Emily might be stirring. She made the tea, and found an unusually pretty porcelain cup, given long ago to her mother, for Emily's tea.

The tea was just as Emily liked it, not too strong and with only a little milk. The steaming fragrance whetted Dolly's own appetite as she bore it upstairs.

She tapped upon the door, but there was no answering call. The cat, which had followed her upstairs, hoping for a comfortable bed, mewed by the closed door.

'I've brought some tea, dear,' called Dolly, opening the door.

Emily was turned away from her, her face towards the window, and the bed-clothes drawn round her motionless figure.

Dolly put the cup carefully upon the bedside table, and walked round the foot of the bed to survey her sleeping friend.

She knew, before her trembling hand touched Emily's cold forehead, that she had been dead for some hours.

* * *

Slowly, Dolly descended the staircase and fumbled her way to a chair. Suddenly, the full weight of her eighty-odd years seemed to crush her. Her heart fluttered in her breast like an imprisoned bird. Her head throbbed dully, and she rested it upon the table before her.

She lay there, felled by the blow, for ten minutes or more. Gradually, her heart quietened and she raised her head. Tears, of which she had not been conscious, had made a damp patch upon the polished surface of the table, and when she raised a hand to her cheek she found it wet with tears which still were running.

She let them flow unchecked, while her strength slowly returned. There was much to be done, but the day was still so young that few people would be astir. For this Dolly was thankful. Her private grief would be unseen, and the last services, which she intended to render her friend, could be undertaken alone.

Dolly Clare had seen death many times in her long life and had prepared her parents for their last journey. She did not flinch from the practical duties which must now be done.

Still trembling, but with quiet courage, she filled a bowl with warm water, collected snowy linen cloths, and returned to the bedroom.

An hour or so later, she locked the house, and walked along the lane to the school house where her friends Mr and Mrs Annett lived.

The leaves were beginning to fall, bright as new pennies on the surface of the road. The mist had gone, and the warmth in the sun was welcomed by Dolly's thin blood.

There was no telephone at the cottage. It was too expensive

an item for the two old friends to install. A public call box was nearer than the Annetts', but Dolly disliked the idea of transmitting her news whilst someone might be waiting outside, an interested witness to her grief.

The school house was peaceful, for the headmaster had just gone across to his duties and was at that moment taking morning prayers, and the two children of the house were also at school.

Mrs Annett took one look at the tall figure, the tear-stained face, and the ineffable air of grief which surrounded the old lady.

'Emily?' she asked swiftly.

Dolly Clare nodded, her lips quivering.

'Sit down, and I'll fetch coffee,' said practical Mrs Annett. But Dolly preferred to follow her hostess into the kitchen. Now that the first shock was wearing away, she felt the need for company.

'I wondered if I might use your telephone,' she said diffidently. 'I should ring Doctor Martin, and then I must make the funeral arrangements.'

'We'll do all that,' said Mrs Annett swiftly. 'Now drink your coffee, and I'll send a message over to the school.'

'You mustn't disturb the time-table,' replied Miss Clare, years of school discipline coming to her aid. But she was overborne.

'It was all very peaceful,' said Dolly. 'I'm sure it was just as Emily had hoped to go. We'd had a perfect last day together, and she went to bed rather tired, but very tranquil and happy.'

'I'm thankful to hear it,' said Mrs Annett, watching the old lady's frail hands twist and turn in her lap, far more poignant than any spoken expression of grief.

'I'm thankful for *everything*,' replied Dolly soberly. 'Our lives have been bound together for so long that we both dreaded prolonged pain and disability for each other. Emily was spared that.'

She rose to go.

'Do stay, please.'

'If you don't mind, I'd sooner be alone. I shall feel better at the cottage, and if you will be so very kind and make all the arrangements I shall be so grateful, my dear. Tell Doctor Martin I shall be waiting for him. No doubt he'll be along after surgery.'

Mrs Annett insisted on walking back with her. She saw her safely installed in her armchair, promised to call again during the day, and returned to make the telephone calls from the school house.

'I wonder,' she thought, as she rustled through the dead leaves at the roadside, 'how long she will survive poor Emily?'

The day passed for Dolly as if in a dream. Doctor Martin, that wise old friend, called in the latter part of the morning. He made his examination, noted the tidy body, the brushed hair and the clean linen enfolding Emily's thin frame. This, he knew, was Dolly's handiwork, and his respect for the old lady's courage grew deeper still.

He surveyed Dolly now as he put his certificate upon the mantel-shelf. Her face showed the ravages of grief, but she was as calm and dignified as ever.

'Any good advising you to stay with your sister for a bit?' he queried.

'No good at all,' answered Dolly, with a small smile. 'This is my home. I need it more than ever now.'

'Very well,' said the doctor. 'Go to bed early, and take two of these pills to make sure that you'll sleep.'

She gave him a quizzical look, but did not take the pills from him.

He put them beside the paper on the mantel-shelf.

'Stubborn girl!' he said. 'Well, there they are, anyway. I promise you, they wouldn't hurt a two-year-old.'

'I'll take them if I can't sleep,' said Dolly. 'You're very kind to me.'

'You wouldn't like me to run you along to the Annetts?'

'No, indeed. I must stay here until Emily is taken into Caxley.'

She put her hand upon his arm, and smiled at him.

'My dear, I'm not in the least frightened. Only sad – and then only selfishly, because I shall miss her so. For her, I don't grieve. She always hoped to go first, and I'm glad things fell out so rightly for her. But I must stay with her until she goes. You understand?'

The doctor nodded, patting the frail hand upon his coat sleeve, then went his way. She might be old, she might be frail, but she had a strength of spirit which out-matched his own, and this the doctor recognised.

In the afternoon, the great black car arrived from the Caxley undertaker's, and four dark-clad men carried Emily down the little staircase and out into the mellow September sunshine. Mute, dry-eyed, Dolly watched them go.

Neighbours called, unhappy and diffident, seeking to help and to offer sympathy. Dolly met them all with sweetness and dignity, but refused to be led from her cottage. Compassion she appreciated: companionship, as yet, she must refuse.

At last, as the sun sank behind the downs, she found herself truly alone. Who would have thought that so much could have happened in the course of twenty-four hours?

This time yesterday, she and Emily had walked back from the oak tree to the shelter of their shared home. She thought of that evening – aeons ago, it seemed – when they had knitted and talked, and shared the company of the crackling fire and the purring cat.

It was another world – but Death had shattered it. She took a deep breath, and walked to the window.

The rooks were flying home. The downs were deep blue against the gold of the sunset. Emily's stocks were already beginning to scent the evening air, and in the distance Dolly could hear the coughing of the one afflicted sheep.

Life went on. No matter what happened, life went on, inexorably, callously, it might seem, to those in grief. But somehow, in this continuity, there were the seeds of comfort.

Dolly returned to the table, took out writing paper and began to draft an entry for *The Caxley Chronicle*.

DAVIS: *On September 20th, at Beech Green, Emily, aged* 84. *Funeral* 2.30 *p.m. Beech Green, Saturday, September 25th.*

She looked at it carefully, checking the notice for any mistakes as meticulously as she had corrected her pupils' work for so many years.

She put it into an envelope, stamped it, and put it on the window sill for the postman to take in the morning.

The house was deathly quiet. She looked about her automatically before mounting the stairs. Doctor Martin's two pills remained untouched, and she ignored them now. She had no heart to warm milk for herself, as she usually did at this hour, and could not trouble to put on a light.

In the darkness she ascended the stairs, comfortless and friendless. She undressed, shivering, and crept into her cold bed.

She had never felt so alone and forlorn, and the night stretched before her, black, bleak and hopeless.

Could she go on, she asked herself? Without Emily?

3 Manny Back's Marrow

WITHOUT Emily!

The words still beat in Dolly Clare's mind as the dawn broke, and she rose thankfully, glad to leave behind the wretchedness of a sleepless night.

She went about her early morning tasks automatically. She felt unusually weak and, grief apart, realised that lack of nourishment was partly the reason. She had been unable to eat the day before. Now she boiled an egg for herself, and cut a thin slice of brown bread and butter for her breakfast. She must look after herself.

There was no trace of self-pity in this observation. Sensible, as always, Dolly now faced the fact that she was quite alone, and if she wished to maintain her independence, which was so dear to her, then she must take care of herself, both in body and mind.

Emily was in her thoughts constantly during the day. Memories of Emily came flooding back. Small incidents, long forgotten, swam into her consciousness, as if to compensate her for the loss of Emily's physical presence.

The name itself had been dear to her for as long as she could remember, for the first Emily in Dolly's life had been a heavy, cumbersome, rag doll, stuffed hard with horse-hair, and much battered about its painted face.

It had been Dolly's companion from babyhood. The doll

Emily was lugged about the little house in Caxley where Dolly was born, bumped upstairs, thrown down them, taken in Dolly's high wicker-work pram on the shopping expeditions in Caxley High Street, and accompanied her young owner to bed each night.

When Dolly was six, the family moved to Beech Green, to the cottage in which she was to live for the rest of her life. Of course, Emily was put into the waggonette which carried their furniture. But a dreadful misfortune occurred on the way.

Emily, who had been propped up in an armchair, the better to see the passing landscape on this great adventure, was jogged by the rough road, fell out, and lay for many days hidden by bushes.

Young Dolly was heart-broken. Even her joy in the new home was dimmed by this catastrophe.

Francis Clare, her father, who was the local thatcher, discovered Emily at last and, full of relief, handed her back to his tearful daughter.

But, somehow, Emily had changed. Rough weather had faded her beauty. Her paint was washed away here and there, and the battered face had become more battered still, so that there was a sinister wryness about Emily's looks which chilled Dolly's ardour.

It was true that Emily was still looked after. She was dressed carefully, and put to bed at night time, but now she slept in a doll's bed and not in her mistress's. Emily had changed, and Dolly mourned for the old Emily she had loved and lost.

Doubly heartening was it then to encounter the second Emily – the small dark girl with eyes as bright as a squirrel's, who took timid Dolly under her wing and made sure that no school bully approached her charge. From that first meeting the friendship had flourished, growing in strength as the years passed.

Dolly was always the quieter of the two. There was a tom-boy element about Emily, encouraged no doubt by her lively brothers who dared her to face exploits which she would not have essayed on her own. It was a high-spirited family, dominated by their mother, a busy little Jenny-wren of a woman.

Dolly found the boys' society overwhelming at first. At home, there was only Ada, her senior by two years, as play-mate. She was a sturdy headstrong child, with a healthy beauty which Dolly envied. Ada was soon elected as queen of the school playground. For her, the boys were creatures who must pay homage.

Dolly looked upon them differently. It was not long before she came to appreciate the humour and honesty, first of the Davis boys, and later of most of her male school fellows. Later still, when she began to teach, she found she had to guard against this secret sympathy with the boys' point of view. She liked their directness of response. If she had occasion to repri-mand a boy, there was usually a posy brought the next day as a peace-offering, and then the whole affair was over.

When a girl needed correction Miss Clare often found that the results were far more complex. There might be no sign given of resentment or guilt. Very often there was a show of bravado instead. But sometimes a mother would appear, with tales of nights spent weeping, or a daughter reluctant to attend school. Certainly, Dolly Clare soon learnt that boys and girls often react differently to the same treatment, and the Davis' household was a sound training ground for her future experience.

All the Davises had a strong sense of justice and fair play. In Emily this quality was allied to an impish sense of humour which led her into many an escapade.

The case of Manny Back was one of them. Although it had occurred more than seventy years ago, Dolly Clare recalled it clearly, and with amusement.

Manny Back had been christened Mansfield Back by his loving parents because Mansfield was the town where their courtship had taken place. Manny was the only pledge of their union, and hopelessly spoilt.

He was a big child. When Dolly Clare first met him at Beech Green School, he sat in one of the senior pupils' desks which had been moved to the junior section of the big schoolroom to accommodate his bulk.

He was not bad-looking in a florid, massive fashion, and his clothes were superior to those of his raggle-taggle neighbours. In the latter years of good Queen Victoria's reign, large families were normal, and clothes were passed down from big brother to the next in line, or cut down from father's, for money was short and, in any case, thrift and ingenuity were looked upon as virtues. A neat patch here and there, or an exquisite darn, were signs of industry as well as poverty. There were plenty of both in Beech Green.

But Manny, as an only child, fared better than most. His father was a boot-maker, and although he did not actually supply all the beautiful riding boots worn by the horse-riding gentlemen of the district, he was generally entrusted with their repair which he did very satisfactorily.

His wife had been laundry maid in good service. Together they saw to it that their only sprig was well-shod and his clothes immaculate.

As much care was lavished on the boy's diet, which was unfortunate for Manny. Whereas the village children carried a homegrown apple, a plum or two, or even a couple of young carrots or some radishes as the seasons supplied them, for their morning 'stay-bit', young Manny would produce a bar of chocolate or a slice of plum-cake for his.

Like most of his fellow-pupils, he ran home for his midday meal and there received much larger and much richer helpings than they could afford. The results were predictable.

Grossly over-weight, Manny soon became the butt of his school-fellows' teasing. A strong streak of savagery runs through every child. Beech Green children, at the end of the last century, could be particularly cruel when roused. After all, it was only the toughest that survived in those days. Weaklings died in infancy, or soon fell prey to consumption, diphtheria and other diseases as yet unconquered by medical science. Those who remained were further toughened by a constant fight against poor food, poor housing, and the stark necessity of competing for work.

Jealousy, no doubt, added to the children's dislike of Manny Back. It is hard to watch a luscious slice of cake vanishing into an already over-sized face when one has only the heel of a stale loaf to satisfy the gnawing pains of youthful hunger. It is hard to see one's fellow-pupil sitting at ease in warm well-fitting boots whilst the damp chill of worn-out soles enflame one's own chilblains.

Manny took his teasing fairly well in the playground, but it was asking too much of human nature for the insults to be ignored completely. Consequently, he vented his outraged feelings on younger children on the way home.

It was unfortunate for Dolly that Manny's house lay beyond her own and that she soon became one of his favourite victims. Fearful of violence, and bewildered by this surprising animosity, poor Dolly began to dread the passage homeward. She watched the great clock on the schoolroom wall with increasing agitation as the hands crept round to four o'clock.

When they stood to sing their grace before leaving, Dolly's folded hands trembled.

'Lord, keep us safe this night,
Secure from all our fears,
May angels guard us while we sleep,
Till morning light appears.
Amen.'

She sang desperately, longing for the angels to be on guard on the homeward way. After all, she reasoned, her parents and Ada could guard her while she slept. Far better to have some assistance, heavenly or otherwise, to withstand Manny's attentions.

If the older Davis boys accompanied her, then Manny did not dare to approach, but more often than not they joined forces with others of their age and vanished on their own ploys in the woods and fields. Emily's presence was a comfort, but no real safeguard from attack. She put up a good fight, using fists, feet and even teeth if necessary, but Manny's bulk could easily overpower her.

Not that Manny took to fighting very often. His methods were more subtle. He was cunning enough to realise that parents would dismiss tale-telling about teasing on the way home. Actual physical harm – a bruise or scratch – might bring a furious parent to his door.

His ways were sly. He would tweak off a hair-ribbon, and hold it too high to be reached by a tearful little girl dreading a mother's wrath. He would threaten the two with stinging nettles. Once, on a hot summer's afternoon, he stirred a wasps' nest, deep in the bank, sending an enraged swarm to follow the girls whilst he escaped over the fields to his house.

He had managed to collect a number of filthy and blasphemous epithets which would have made his devoted parents' hair rise, had they heard him using them. Dolly and Emily found them shocking, and said so. Manny, needless to say, was only encouraged by his success, and used them all the more.

All in all, Manny Back was a menace to Dolly's happiness and, short of telling tales, which she had no intention of doing, there seemed to be no way in which she could take action.

But Emily did.

A day or two after the incident of the wasps, and while her arm still smarted with the stings, Emily vowed vengeance.

'It's not fair!' she said indignantly to Dolly. 'Not fair!'

'But what can we do?'

'I've thought of something to pay him back.'

'Oh Emily,' quavered Dolly, 'it will only make him worse.'

Emily's face took on a look of grim determination, but her eyes sparkled.

'I'll teach him,' said Emily.

'What will you do?' asked Dolly fearfully.

Emily surveyed her timorous friend.

'I shan't tell you,' she announced, 'because you'd be upset, and maybe tell your mum.'

'I *wouldn't*!' shouted Dolly, much hurt by this slur on her integrity.

'Well, all the same, I'm keeping it to myself,' said Emily, a trifle smugly. 'You'll know in good time.'

She began to laugh, and danced dizzily about the playground, her dark plaits bouncing. Dolly, recognising defeat, watched her friend rejoicing in her secret, and trembled for her future downfall.

It was the custom at that time at Beech Green School, for the boys to cultivate a large kitchen garden.

It was worked communally, under Mr Finch's keen eye, and the vegetables were bought very cheaply by the boys. By the side of the communal patch lay a narrower strip, divided into a dozen or so small plots, for any boy who wanted to till a little garden of his own, providing his own seeds or plants.

Manny owned one of these, and had devoted the entire plot to the growing of marrows. Perhaps it was the affinity between the bulbous marrows and his own stoutness which made Manny's marrows grow so remarkably well. They certainly throve, and Manny plied them with manure and rainwater and watched them swell into sleek striped maturity.

The pick of the crops from the school garden went to the Beech Green flower show in September. The school had a special display, and it was considered a great honour to have something on show for parents and friends to admire. Manny was determined to put in his largest marrow.

There was one in particular which was his pride. It was dark and glossy, with a sheen on it like satin, and it was destined to be a perfect beauty. Beside its splendour, its striped brothers looked positively peaky although, in truth, they were very fine specimens as marrows go.

Early in its life, Manny had taken a stout darning needle and scratched his name neatly along its side.

MANSFIELD BACK it said, in tidy capitals, and as the weeks passed the letters grew larger and plainer as the marrow increased in girth. Manny had no doubt that it would be chosen for display, and the thought of his signature emblazoned there for all Beech Green to see and admire gave him the keenest satisfaction.

After the show, the school's produce was carried to the church for Harvest Festival which always took place on the Sunday following the show day. With any luck, thought Manny, his marrow would be placed in the porch, or perhaps below the pulpit, there to dazzle the eyes of the devout.

Later still, the produce would be taken to Caxley hospital, there to be devoured by properly-grateful patients. The thought of his marrow being assailed by a sharp knife, plunged into boiling water, and finally eaten, gave Manny acute pain. He turned his mind from the marrow's ultimate fate and concentrated instead on the glory which was to be his.

One evening, just as dusk was falling, a small figure might have been seen, entering the school garden through a hedge at the rear. It advanced stealthily through the gathering gloom and knelt down among Manny's marrows.

A small hand, bearing a penknife, lifted the vine-shaped leaves beneath which the prize beauty lay hidden. For three or four breathless minutes, dreadful work went on in the silent garden.

Then, back through the hedge crept Emily, revenged and unrepentant.

A week of heavy rain followed, and Manny had no need to pay much attention to his marrow bed. It was some ten days later that he went to water the beauties and, as he was in some hurry, on that occasion, he did not disturb the leaves which covered the prize exhibit. The dark glossy end protruded like the polished barrel of a cannon. At this rate of growth, it should be the largest marrow in the whole show, let alone on the school stall. Manny's spirits were jubilant.

Four days later, whilst he was digging with his fellows on the communal patch, two breathless children rushed up to him.

'Seen yer marrer, Man?'

Manny looked at them with distaste. There was a gloating excitement about them which made him apprehensive.

'What's up with it?'

'Someone's bin and written on it.'

'I know that,' said Manny huffily. 'I scratched my name on it weeks ago.'

'It ain't just yer name,' retorted one of the boys. He waved his arm expansively, beckoning the group to come and see for themselves.

Mr Finch had gone into school for a few minutes leaving the boys to get on alone. Carrying forks and hoes, the boys now drifted across the private plots.

The more vociferous of the two discoverers knelt down by Manny's marrow and lifted the leaves aside.

There, plain for all to see, were the words:

MANSFIELD BACK

and below, in smaller capitals the one word:

BULLY

Grins split the faces of the watching boys as they observed Manny's face. It changed from pink to scarlet, then faded to a greyish pallor. And then, to everyone's horror, Manny burst into tears.

'And what,' said Mr Finch, returning, 'is the meaning of this? Get back to your work.'

'Please, sir,' said the vociferous one, 'somethinks happened to Manny's marrer.'

Mr Finch's sharp eye fell upon the tearful owner.

'Let me see, boy.'

Snuffling, shaken with sobs, Manny parted the leaves and displayed the outrage. Mr Finch looked stern. He then bent down to finger the added word BULLY.

'Done recently,' he said. 'Within the last week or two.'

He straightened up and surveyed the little crowd around him.

'Well, come along, boys,' he said peremptorily. 'Own up now. You are the only people to come in this garden. Who's to blame?'

There was an unhappy silence and much foot-shuffling. Manny's sniffs grew more frequent.

'Blow your nose, child,' snapped Mr Finch. Manny unfolded a beautifully clean handkerchief and did as he was bid.

'At once, boys. Who's done this mean thing to Manny?'

'I never,' said one quaking red-head, known as Copperknob.

'Not me,' whispered several more.

Mr Finch's experienced eye travelled over them all. There seemed to be very few guilty looks among them.

'Who's away today?'

'Only Jim Potts, sir. He never done it.'

'And how do you know what Jimmy Potts done? Did?' Mr Finch snapped, correcting himself briskly.

Silence fell again. Mr Finch's moustache was bristling, a sure sign of danger.

'File into school as soon as you have cleaned your tools and put them back,' ordered the headmaster. 'We'll get to the bottom of this.'

Twenty minutes later, after ruthless interrogation, Mr Finch had to admit to himself that the mystery was unsolved. He could only be certain of one thing. These boys, for once in their lives, were innocent.

Most of the schoolchildren had gone home by the time Mr Finch's class were dismissed.

'We'll see about this after prayers first thing tomorrow,' announced the headmaster. 'You may dismiss. But I want you to stay behind, Manny.'

The schoolroom was very quiet as Mr Finch asked a few searching questions. He had heard rumours about Manny's behaviour, but had had no definite evidence of bullying. What he learned from Manny's faltering replies gave him some sympathy with the unknown malefactor. But justice must be done, and would be done in the morning.

Manny, still tearful, made his solitary way homeward, leaving Mr Finch to think about the incident.

What a simple way of getting one's own back, thought the headmaster, as he locked up the cupboards! Manny would be powerless to hide the incriminating word. Any attempt to disguise it would ruin the marrow's beauty. Oh, yes, this was indeed a subtle blow!

Nonetheless, thought Mr Finch, the culprit must be punished. To deface Manny's marrow, on which so much loving care had been lavished, was a cruel trick.

The next morning the whole school remained standing after prayers and heard the sorry tale. There were a few titters which Mr Finch quelled instantly. It was pretty plain that Manny had few supporters.

'Will the boy who did this despicable thing come forward,' said Mr Finch, his eye raking the back rows where the tallest and oldest pupils stood.

'At once!' thundered Mr Finch. 'Or the whole school stays in this afternoon until we get to the bottom of this!'

From the front row, where the smallest children stood, the neat figure of Emily Davis emerged. Her dark head was on a level with the headmaster's watch chain. Her clear grey eyes looked up into his astonished face.

'I cut the word,' said Emily. Her voice was steady.

There was a stir of amusement in the ranks behind her.

'Silence!' roared Mr Finch, and there was.

'Go to your classes,' he ordered. 'And you, Emily Davis, will come with me.'

He led the way into the lobby where the children hung their clothes. Dolly Clare watched Emily's small figure following the headmaster's portly one, looking like a diminutive tug following a liner. What would happen to her in the privacy of the lobby? Dolly trembled for her friend.

She need not have suffered so. Mr Finch was a just man and, after hearing Emily's side of the story, he realized that there had been provocation.

Emily's punishment was to have no play for a week. Whilst the others rushed about the playground, she was to stand by the headmaster's desk contemplating the fearful ends of those who took the law into their own hands. Alas, it was a lesson which Emily Davis never completely learned in life, and injustice was always quick to prick her into action.

As for Manny Back's marrow, it was never displayed. A lesser giant from his marrow bed gained third prize, and with this he had to be content. Dolly Clare and Emily Davis were not molested again by the biggest boy in the school, on their homeward journeys. Mr Finch saw to that.

Years later, looking back on the incident, Dolly Clare wondered if they had not under-estimated Mr Finch's sense of humour which was so successfully hidden under his stern manner.

For could it have been coincidence alone that caused the headmaster to read the story of David and Goliath at assembly next morning?

4 Wartime Memories

IT was not only Emily's keen sense of justice that Dolly Clare remembered, as she moved slowly about the cottage, trying to accustom herself to the numbing sense of loss. Emily had always had courage in abundance.

It had needed courage to step forward and confess to the crime of defacing Manny's marrow. It had needed courage to stand by the headmaster's desk, dry-eyed, whilst the rest of the school played outside in the sunshine. But, to Dolly's mind, Emily's courage was supreme when she faced the darkest hour of her life as a girl in her twenties.

Dolly and Emily, as they grew up, made very few friends. The furthest they went from home was Caxley, where they went to evening classes as part of their teacher-training, or sometimes to shop for things which were unobtainable at the village stores.

Most of the young men had been known to them all their lives, had shared desks with them at the village school, and stirred them no more than a brother would. No one could accuse either Emily or Dolly of being flirtatious: many, in fact, thought them too prosaic and unromantic. Certainly, the flamboyant novelettes, so beloved by some of their contemporaries, did not interest them, and older women, gossiping by the village pump, looked sourly at the two friends when they passed.

'Heads too full o' book-learnin' to find them a husband,' said one, when the girls were out of earshot.

'They'll find themselves on the shelf, them two,' agreed another.

'Too hoity-toity to go out with my Billy as asked 'em to the fair,' added a third. 'Gettin' above themselves with all this teaching nonsense.'

Jealousy was at the root of such remarks. Most of their daughters were in service at twelve years old, or soon after, and to see Dolly and Emily aiming at higher things aroused maternal resentment.

It was not that the two girls were blind to male attractions. They discussed the pros and cons of the young men around as keenly as the other girls of their own age, and probably more wisely. But, whereas most of the girls talked of nothing else but their conquests and their intention of marrying, Emily and Dolly had many other equally absorbing interests. The children they taught, the books they read, the lovely natural things around them which gave them constant joy, engrossed them quite as much as the thought of marriage. Luckily for them, their work was fascinating, not something to escape from, as it was for so many of their over-worked young friends, at the mercy, very often, of dictatorial employers. If Emily and Dolly married, as they calmly assumed that they would do some day, then it would be for a positive cause, not as an escape from tedious or intolerable conditions.

It so happened that the two friends became engaged within a few weeks of each other. Dolly Clare was attracted, at first sight, by the tall young man with red hair who came to be under-gardener at the big house at Beech Green. His name was Arnold Fletcher, and his home was in Norfolk.

There was something exciting about this young man from far away. He was quicker and gayer than the friends of Dolly's youth, and the mere fact that he found his new surroundings stimulating made Dolly look at the old familiar places with a fresh eye. He shared Dolly's love of books and music, and he brought with him a breath of the salty wind which blew so refreshingly about his native Norfolk. Their engagement was considered an excellent thing, even by the most curmudgeonly of the village folk.

Emily's choice was a local farmer's son. His name was Edgar Bennett and his father and grandfather had been tenant farmers at Springbourne, a neighbouring village, for many years.

Edgar was as tall as Dolly's Arnold, but his colouring was pale. He had ashen-fair hair, and the clear grey eyes which so often go with it. He was a quiet, gentle fellow, and the general feeling was that Emily's drive and vivacity would 'put some life' into him.

He was the eldest son and it seemed likely that he would carry on the farm when his father gave up. Two younger sons were in business in Caxley, and it looked as though Emily would live eventually in the sturdy four-square Georgian farm house set in a hollow on the flanks of the downs.

But to begin with, the young couple were to make their home in a cottage near the boundary of the Bennetts' farm and that of Harold Miller who owned the Hundred Acre field hard by the Clares' cottage.

Dolly and Emily planned to have their weddings in the autumn of 1914. By that time, Edgar would have helped to bring in the harvest and there would be a break before winter ploughing began.

But these plans were made in the spring, a few months before the outbreak of war with Germany shattered their hopes.

'Better postpone it,' said Arnold to Dolly sadly.

'We'll all be back by Christmas,' said Edgar to Emily, consoling her.

The two young men went to Caxley to enlist, one bright August day, waving from a farm wagon, crowded with fresh-faced country boys going on the same errand.

Dolly and Emily were heavy-hearted, but saw the sense of a postponement of their plans. Far better to continue steadily with their teaching while their men were away. Everyone said it would be over before long. Perhaps a spring wedding would be better still?

They were false hopes indeed. Far from being over by Christmas, as the confident had boasted, it was quite apparent, by that time, that the war could drag on indefinitely.

In February, when the year was at its coldest and most cheerless, Dolly came home from school one day to find a tear-stained letter from Arnold's parents, telling her that they had heard of his death in action. Dolly's first reaction was complete disbelief.

Someone as loving and alive as Arnold could not possibly be snuffed out like a candle flame! This was some cruel mistake. It could not be right.

It was the stricken look on her parents' faces which finally brought home to her the awful truth. Even then she could not cry, but went about her affairs, numbed with grief, in a dreadful strange calm which frightened those about her.

It was at this time of her life that Dolly felt the full strength of Emily's support. Her sympathy took a practical turn. She brought her a bunch of violets to smell, or a bottle of home-made wine to tempt her listless appetite. She persuaded Dolly to accompany her on quiet walks where the gentle sounds of trees and birds could act as a balm to her friend's torn spirits.

Emily said little about Arnold's death, unlike so many neighbours, meaning well, who poured sympathy into Dolly's ears but only succeeded in torturing the girl and distressing themselves. The fear that Edgar too might die, was constantly with Emily, but she gave no sign of it to Dolly. Outwardly, she remained cheerful and loving, and Dolly, looking back later, realised just how bravely and generously Emily gave all her strength to comfort her. There was an unselfishness and nobility about Emily, at this time, far beyond her years.

A more cruel blow was in store for Emily. One spring day, when the high clouds scudded across the blue sky above the downs, and the lambs skipped foolishly below, an urgent message came from Edgar who was fighting in France. It said simply: 'For God's sake send me a gas mask.'

The two bewildered girls had done their best with cotton wool and tape to design some poor defence against this unknown method of warfare. Together they had taken the precious parcel to Caxley, cycling through the balmy evening air filled with the music of the blackbirds' song, so that it should go by the quickest possible post from the main office in Caxley High Street.

They heard that Edgar received it, but the gas attacks continued relentlessly. Some weeks later, Edgar returned from France, a victim of gas, and was sent to a hospital, not far from Bournemouth, for long months of recovery.

Emily took the blow well. She was now headmistress of the tiny school at Springbourne, for the headmaster had enlisted as soon as war broke out. Despite the hard work which this involved, Emily made the long journey to see Edgar every week-end, staying overnight in cheap lodgings near the hospital gates.

Edgar was a wraith of his former self. His eyes looked huge in his pale wasted face, and the terrible coughing attacks, which tore his damaged lungs, tore just as cruelly at Emily's heart-strings.

But Edgar's welcome and his joy in her presence were worth every minute of the long journey. She stayed with him until the last train each Sunday, and it was often past midnight when she reached home to fall exhausted into bed.

Throughout the dismal winter Emily continued to make her journeys, and now it was Dolly's turn to be comforter. Once or twice she accompanied Emily, but she could not afford to make the trip very often. Emily herself had foregone a new winter coat and boots to pay the fare each weekend, and Dolly had insisted on giving her money as a Christmas present, so that she could visit Edgar as often as possible.

Gradually, Edgar improved. They made their marriage plans anew. Now they would have a summer wedding.

Edgar was moved to a convalescent home not far from the hospital. It was an easier journey for Emily, with one less change by railway.

She was as blithe as a summer bird as the days grew longer. She and Dolly set about preparing the cottage which had been waiting empty for so long.

The two girls spent the long light evenings distempering the walls and scrubbing out cupboards and floors. There were wide serene views from the cottage windows, looking down over the sloping downs dotted with the sheep of Edgar's farm. They would perch on the wooden window seat or on upturned buckets in the porch, and revel in the last rays of the sun as they rested from their labours. Sometimes, they took a simple meal of cheese and biscuits and would sit outside, their hair lifted by the soft breeze, gazing at the view which would soon be Emily's daily one.

These busy, but tranquil, hours did much to restore Dolly's spirits, and her own sense of loss was lessened by Emily's bubbling happiness. It was plain that Edgar would never be fit for active service again. As soon as he was released from the convalescent home he would return to the farm to work as best he could. His future, it seemed, held no more war-like excursions, and Dolly rejoiced for her friend.

Doubly bitter was it then when the blow fell. One evening of golden sunlight, only a few weeks before the appointed wedding day, Dolly arrived at the cottage to find Emily sitting with a letter on her lap, and tears rolling down her cheeks.

She handed the letter to Dolly without a word. It was a short note from Edgar stating baldly that he had fallen in love with one of the nurses and that they planned to marry as soon as possible.

'I don't deserve you anyway' the letter ended. How true that was! thought Dolly, putting her arms round Emily's shaking frame.

They sat thus for hours it seemed, while the sun grew lower and the sheep's distant cries came to them through the open windows.

At last, Emily rose and left the house, followed by Dolly. She locked the front door and put the key and the letter together into her belt.

'Emily?' questioned Dolly, searching her friend's resolute face for an answer.

'He's made his choice,' said Emily, taking a deep breath. 'I'll abide by it.'

'But won't you try and see him?' asked Dolly.

'Never!' said Emily. 'It's her house now. I can't bear to look at it ever again.'

From that day Emily Davis had done her best never to look upon the little cottage where she had dreamed of happiness. It was Dolly and Mrs Davis who had removed Emily's curtains and the few pieces of furniture which were already put into the downstairs rooms.

It was they who disposed of them, for Emily would have nothing to do with this bitter clearing-up. The wounds were too fresh and raw to bear this added salt rubbed into them. For a time, she spoke to no one about the tragedy, but gradually she brought herself to say a little to Dolly, and as the months and years passed, Emily faced life without Edgar with a courage which was typical.

Only Dolly guessed how deeply Emily was wounded by this affair. Edgar married his nurse one July day of thunderstorms and torrential rain. Maybe it was augury, thought Dolly, for the years that followed were stormy ones indeed for Edgar. He had married a virago, it turned out, and despite three bonny children there was little happiness in the cottage on the downs, and later in the farmhouse which they took over at his father's death.

There was no doubt in Dolly's mind that Emily's tragedy was far more difficult to bear than her own. Edgar lived in the same small community, his marriage under constant scrutiny by his neighbours. Emily was forced, throughout her long life, to keep a still tongue and a calm face when informed of Edgar's doings.

Her love for him never wavered. It was the kind of love, Dolly often thought, which one read of in old ballads, where the woman was called upon to endure all manner of humiliations and tests before her lord would acknowledge her. But in ballads, this faithful love was rewarded. Emily's was not.

The fact that Edgar's marriage was a miserable one added to her unhappiness. Her spirit was too fine to find consolation in the 'I-told-you-so' attitude of many of her neighbours. It was no comfort to Emily to know that Edgar had chosen wrongly, but only an added tragedy.

She did her best to avoid meeting him, sometimes going some distance afield to miss him at work on the farm. Never, if she could help it, would she pass the cottage. But, one day, some eight or nine years after his marriage, she met him face to face unexpectedly, and they spoke a few words. She told Dolly about this encounter many years later.

She was walking up a rough cart track which led to the top of the downs. Spindleberries grew at the edge of a little copse on the chalky lower slopes, and she was on her way to collect some for a nature study lesson next day. Suddenly, there was a crackling of twigs from the copse, and Edgar emerged, holding a gun. He drew in his breath sharply.

'I'm sorry, Emily. Hope I didn't scare you. I'm after jays.'

Emily, speechless, shook her head.

He leant his gun against the green-rimed trunk of an elder tree and came towards her. She looked steadily into his face, and what she saw there made her start to run.

He caught her arm, and looked sadly and longingly into her eyes.

'Oh, Emily,' he said, 'what a mess I've made of it!'

'Edgar, please,' protested Emily. 'This will do no good.' She struggled to get away but he held her arm firmly.

'Hear me for one minute.'

Emily stood still. She was more stirred than she could believe. That steadfast love, which had never wavered, was now mingled with pity for the unhappy man before her.

'I made the mistake of my life when I chose Eileen. Life's hell. I'm not complaining – I brought it on myself. But when the gossips tell you tit-bits about our cat-and-dog life, Em, you can multiply it by a hundred.'

'So bad?' whispered Emily, shaken.

'So bad,' repeated Edgar. He released her arm and turned away.

'I'm sorry – *truly* sorry,' said Emily. 'You deserve happiness after all you went through in the war. But, Edgar, try not to speak to me again.'

Her lips quivered, and the elder tree, and the gun, and the man were blurred by the tears which filled her eyes.

He turned towards her, and Emily saw that tears too were on his cheek.

'*Please,*' cried Emily, 'because – can't you see? I just can't bear it!'

And, weeping, she stumbled back the way which she had come, leaving him there, forlorn.

Poor Emily, thought Dolly Clare. And poor Edgar, now an old, old man. How would he face the news of Emily's death? Did he still remember the girl whom he had once loved, so many years ago?

5 Edgar Hears the News

EDGAR Bennett sat in the September sunlight and surveyed his gnarled old hands ruefully. The dratted joints were more swollen than ever! Fat lot of good that doctor's muck had done him!

He had once been proud of those hands, now mottled with the brown stains of old age. They had held a plough steady all day long, wielded a scythe, harnessed scores of horses, and used a cricket bat, with such skill, that at least one century from Edgar Bennett, each season, was celebrated at Beech Green in the old days.

Now they were fit for nothing but pulling on his clothes each morning, and then with pain, or peeling the confounded potatoes that Eileen put before him every day.

'No need to sit idle,' she said sharply to him. 'Just because you can't get about as you used to, it don't follow that you're helpless.'

He looked at them now, swimming about in a bowl of muddy water on the bench beside him. He sat in an old wooden armchair which had been his father's, close by the back door of the farm house.

It was a sheltered spot, and whenever the weather was fine, Edgar struggled out there with the aid of his stick and looked across the fields which he had sown and tended until ill-health had forced him to retire, two or three years ago.

His son John ran the farm now, and lived in the main part of the farm house. Edgar and Eileen had the old kitchen and two other rooms downstairs for their quarters, and the old dairy had been turned into a bathroom.

One way and another, thought Edgar, listening to the distant combine churring round the farm's largest field, they were pretty lucky. No stairs to worry about, for one thing, but no one knew how much he missed the glorious view of the downs from the window of the main bedroom. It had never failed to hearten him – in good weather or bad.

The fruit trees in the garden obscured the vista, and now Edgar's horizon was bounded by the hawthorn hedge which enclosed the farm garden. It was all pretty enough, he supposed, looking with lack-lustre eye at the dahlias and early Michaelmas daisies which John's wife Annie tended so zealously; but it was not a patch on the rolling downs, undulating as far as the eye could see, filling a man with wonder and awe.

He sighed, and fished in the bowl of water for the first potato. His right hand held an ancient steel knife with a horn handle. It had been new when he and Eileen married at the end of the First World War. Now, the blade was broken short, and it had come down to kitchen work. Edgar found it comfortable to manage with his twisted fingers.

He peeled carefully, getting the parings as thin as possible. Eileen was a stickler for wasting nothing. Even the eyes must be gouged out with the least possible waste. It was a ticklish job, thought Edgar, bending over his task in the sunlight.

And one which Eileen had always hated, he remembered. When she had given up her nursing to marry him she made it clear that cooking was a penance to her. Housework she enjoyed. Her training as a nurse made her standards of cleanliness uncommonly high – too dratted uncomfortably high, Edgar said – and the farm house gleamed from every surface capable of being polished. The place reeked of cleaning materials. If it wasn't bees-wax on the furniture, it was methylated spirits from the rag which cleaned the windows, or the breath-catching pungency of the bleaching liquid which Eileen liked to use for the sink and drains.

Now that the house was mainly in Annie's hands, it smelt less like an institution and more like a home, thought Edgar. The smell of baking pervaded the house. Vases of roses or narcissi, or wallflowers – or whatever fragrant blooms were in season in the garden – gave out their own sweetness. It did not please Eileen.

'Everlasting petals all over the place,' she grumbled to Edgar. 'Messy things, flowers. Spoil the polish.'

'I like 'em,' said Edgar mildly. 'And in any case, Annie's entitled to do what she likes in her own home. Some young women would have turned us out. In-laws don't make the best house-mates, you know.'

Eileen snorted. There was small chance of getting Edgar to take her side, as well she knew. From the very first days of marriage she had discovered that, despite his gentle ways and apparent submissiveness, there was an obstinate streak in Edgar's character. She, who loved to rule, found that there were some occasions when her husband stood fast. Her temper was fiery, her voice shrill. Neither improved with age, but Edgar had grown used to these outbursts, treating them with a stubborn silence which drove Eileen to even greater fury.

Luckily, the three children had inherited their father's nature. In some ways, it made matters even worse for Eileen, for there was no one to answer her with equal fire. Her sharp tongue met little verbal resistance. John, the eldest, went so far as to laugh at his mother's tantrums as he grew to manhood, and his easy attitude did much to help his wife Annie to be philosophical about the old people's presence in the house.

'I'd put up with anything for the old man,' John said. 'He bears the brunt of it, poor old chap. Don't hurt us to have 'em here, if we act sensible, and I'm not seeing my mum and dad turned out of their home at their age.'

The two younger boys, equally mild-mannered, worked in Caxley and were both married. Sometimes they came out on a Sunday afternoon to see the old people, but they did not visit very often, and as neither enjoyed letter-writing, Eileen and Edgar heard little of them, despite their presence within five miles of the farm.

'All the same, children,' Eileen said tartly. 'Ungrateful lot. You brings 'em up and gets no thanks for it.'

'Didn't ask to come, did 'em?' replied Edgar. 'You be thankful they ain't turned out jail-birds or worse. We've got three fine boys, all doing well. What more d'you want?'

Looking back, turning the wet potato in his swollen fingers, Edgar wondered how many days of his marriage had passed without some outburst from Eileen. God, she was a nagger, if ever there was one! What madness had made him take her on in the first place?

A shadow fell across his armchair, and he looked up to see Tom More, the postman. He held out a letter.

'Shouldn't bother to open it,' he remarked. 'Looks like a bill.'

'You been through 'em all?' asked Edgar jocularly. 'Any good news?'

'No,' said Tom, settling on the bench near the bowl of potatoes. 'Got a bit of bad, though.'

'Oh? What's up?'

'Poor old Emily Davis.'

Edgar drew in his breath sharply. Tom More was too young to know what Emily meant to him, but he bent over the knife in his hand so that his face was hidden.

'She's gone,' continued Tom. 'Saw Dolly Clare half an hour back. She said they took their evening toddle up the field, had some supper and Emily was as right as rain at bed-time.

'Next morning she found her dead in bed.'

'I'm sorry,' said Edgar huskily. 'Very sorry. She was at school with me.'

There was a pause. From a distance the hum of the combine continued. Close at hand, one of the farm cats came round the corner of the house, mewing plaintively.

'How's Dolly Clare taken it? She got anyone there with her?'

'Seems all right. Looks a bit pale-like. I heard she was asked to go up Annetts' place, but she said "No".'

'Home's best at times like that,' agreed Edgar. His voice was shaky, and Tom More noticed that his hands shook too. These old people never liked to hear of their generation dying. Brought it too near home, no doubt. Maybe he shouldn't have told the old boy.

He shifted uneasily, and gave a gusty sigh.

'Ah well, must be getting along. You're looking very fit, Edgar. See us all out, you will. 'Morning, now.'

He ambled off towards the gate, hoping that he had made amends with his last remarks. Must be rotten, getting old, thought Tom, turning for a final wave at the gate.

Edgar was still bent over his task. But the shaky hands were not working, and Edgar's gaze was not upon the potato he now held, but upon a vision of Emily Davis, a life-time ago, as he remembered her.

The first time that Emily had come to Edgar's notice was on the occasion of her confession at school assembly. Edgar had been standing in the back row, among the oldest boys at Beech Green school, due to leave in a few months for the waiting world of hard work.

The affair of Manny's marrow had amused them. Mr Finch's threat of keeping in the whole school did not. He was a man who kept his word, and Edgar and his school-mates had too many activities to attend to after school to welcome any restriction of their liberty.

It was with relief then, as well as amusement, that the bigger boys saw little Emily Davis step out to take her punishment.

'Got some spunk that little 'un,' one boy had commented, as they filed out.

'All them Davises have,' said another. It was something which Edgar was to find out for himself years later.

Emily Davis did not cross his path again for some time. He saw her occasionally about the village, usually in the company of Dolly Clare, but she meant nothing to him. He was busy on the farm, and his only relaxation was the cricket which he played on summer Saturday afternoons whenever the work on the farm allowed.

But one autumn evening, when the beech trees were ablaze on the road to Caxley, and the blue smoke of autumn bonfires drifted through the village, Edgar encountered Emily.

It had been a good harvest that year, and Edgar had taken

a wagon laden with sacks of wheat to Caxley Station. When the wagon was empty, he had reloaded it with sacks of coal, ready for the winter, and set off on the return journey. He was pleasantly tired after the heavy work, and looking forward to an evening meal and early bed.

Perched high on the plank seat at the front of the wagon, he had a fine view of the surrounding countryside.

The fruit trees in the cottage gardens were weighed down with apples and plums. In one garden, a cottager was bent over his rows of bronze onions, turning the tops for final ripening. In another, a woman was tending a bonfire of dead pea-sticks and dried weeds. Everywhere there were the signs of the dying year, and the nutty fragrance of autumn hung in the air.

'Soon be Harvest Festival,' said Edgar aloud to the massive haunches of Daisy, the old cart-horse, moving stolidly along between the shafts. She snorted in reply, and shook her shaggy head. She was a companionable animal, and liked the sound of a human voice.

The thought of Manny's marrow, destined never to be the centre-piece of a Harvest Festival, flashed back to Edgar. It was the first time he had remembered it for years, and he savoured the memory now, as Daisy descended the steep hill leading to distant Beech Green.

At the bottom, there was a sharp bend, and as Daisy rounded it, she pulled suddenly to one side.

'Whoa there!' said Edgar, startled. 'All right, old girl!'

On the verge, at the side of the road, knelt Emily Davis beside a bicycle. Her small hands were black, her hair dishevelled, and her hat hung from a spray of yellowing hawthorn in the hedge.

'What's up then?' asked Edgar, leaping down.

'The chain's come off,' said Emily.

'Here, you hold it upright,' ordered Edgar, 'and I'll have a go.'

Emily struggled to her feet, and did as she was told; Daisy wandered towards the grass and browsed happily, tearing great mouthfuls and munching noisily.

'Funny thing,' said Edgar. 'I was thinking about you.'

'Honest?' said Emily surprised. 'What about me?'

'Manny's marrow.'

Emily flushed and looked disconcerted.

'Oh that!' she said discomfited. 'I try and forget that. It was a mean trick really, but that boy got my dander up.'

'You did all right,' said Edgar robustly. He lifted the back wheel from the gritty road and spun it swiftly.

'This chain's pretty slack,' he observed. 'Tell you what. You climb up with me and we'll put the old grid on the back. Can't do much to that chain without some tools, and if you ride it like it is, then ten to one it'll be off again in a hundred yards.'

'Thanks,' said Emily. He watched her climb up to the front of the wagon, as nimbly as a monkey despite her long skirt. He heaved up the bicycle, lodging it securely between two sacks of coal, and clambered aloft beside her.

'Come up, Daisy!' he commanded, and the old horse left her meal reluctantly and clip-clopped steadily towards home.

'Where've you been then?' asked Edgar, making conversation.

'Caxley. At evening class. You have to, you know, while you're a pupil teacher.

'D'you like it?'

'Teaching? Yes, I do – better now than when I started. Are you still with your father?'

'Yes. And I'll stay that way, I reckon. I'll take over the farm gradually, I expect, when he gets past it. Not that there's any sign of that yet. He's a tough old party, thank God.'

They jogged along peaceably. The air was growing chilly as the sun slipped down behind the downs.

'Do you go to Caxley much?' asked Emily, pulling her jacket round her.

'Next trip'll be to the Michaelmas Fair,' said Edgar. He looked at her suddenly. She'd grown into a nice-looking girl, small and neat, with dark hair piled untidily on top of her head. True, she had a black grease mark from the bicycle chain on one cheek, but it didn't detract from her charms, to Edgar's appraising eye.

'What about coming with me?' urged Edgar. Emily turned wide grey eyes upon him.

'Well, I *was* going with Dolly and my brother Albert,' she began uncertainly.

'Tell you what,' said Edgar. 'Dad'll let me have the little cart, and I'll pick you three up. How's that?'

'That would be lovely!' said Emily, glowing with pleasure. 'You say what time and we'll be ready waiting.'

'Good,' replied Edgar. 'Let's say half past six. I'll be there.'

They drew up at the end of the lane where the Davises lived. Their thatched roof was visible a few yards down the road.

Edgar jumped down and released the bicycle from its lodging place.

'I'll wheel it down for you,' he offered. 'Old Daisy'll wait for me.'

'No, don't you bother,' said Emily hastily. 'It's no distance.

Albert'll be home now, and I'll get him to make the chain safe. And thank you *very* much, Edgar, for the lift, and for helping me.'

'No trouble,' said Edgar. 'I'll look out for you on Saturday week then.'

'It will be lovely,' said Emily, giving him a dazzling smile. My word, thought Edgar, she's getting quite a beauty, is little Emily!

She waved goodbye, and set off down the lane. Edgar watched her until a bend in the road hid her from sight.

'That's a real nice little maid,' observed Edgar to Daisy.

Daisy snorted in agreement and quickened her pace, advancing towards her stable and a good feed. There had been enough dallying—that was her opinion.

6 Edgar and Emily

OLD Edgar put a peeled potato carefully in the saucepan and straightened his legs in the sunshine. He had been to many Michaelmas Fairs since that one with Emily over half a century ago, but it was that particular occasion which stayed so clearly in his memory.

How slowly the days had passed after that first encounter with Emily on the road from Caxley! He had been surprised by the strength of his desire to see her again, and looked forward eagerly to the Saturday evening.

It had gone well, right from the start, he remembered.

His father had given permission willingly for the little cart to be used on the Saturday evening, and had come upon his son, during that afternoon, polishing the brass work on cart and harness with unusual industry. The long black cushions, buttoned and horse-hair stuffed, which ran along each side of the cart were dusted, and the bottom of the cart swept clean.

'Who's the girl?' asked Edgar's father, with a smile.

'I'm picking up Albert Davis and Dolly Clare,' said Edgar, trying to sound casual, and failing utterly.

'And who's to be your lady for the evening?'

'Well,' said Edgar, studying a brass stud closely, 'Emily Davis is coming too.'

'Look after her then,' replied the old man. 'I like the Davises. You treat that girl right, mind.'

'Of course, dad,' said Edgar shortly. The old man continued on his way.

The three were waiting for him at the end of the lane where he had dropped Emily after the bicycle incident. She was dressed in a bright scarlet coat, which showed up her dark hair to advantage. What Dolly wore, Edgar had no idea. His eyes were only for Emily.

The roundabouts and swingboats were close by the statue of Queen Victoria in the market square at Caxley. She looked faintly disapproving, standing there among the cheerful vulgarity of the fair.

Naphtha lights flared, music blared away, children screamed as they careered round and round on the galloping horses, and the stall-holders shouted their attractions with lungs of brass. The din was unbelievable. After sampling all the side-shows, and having taken two trips on the roundabout and switchback, Emily begged to be allowed to stand still for a few minutes to calm her whirling senses. Dolly and Albert were high in a swing-boat above them.

'Come down to the river for a minute,' said Edgar, leading the way, and Emily was glad to obey.

After the tumult of the market square, the riverside was cool and quiet. A little breeze rustled the autumn leaves, and Emily welcomed the refreshing air on her hot face. They leant companionably, side by side, on the bridge, and watched the placid Cax slipping gently along below them, gleaming dully like pewter in the night light. Somewhere nearby, a splash told of a moorhen or water-rat going about its business. The distant racket of the fair was muted and the native sounds of water and trees in harmony made the age-old music of the night.

Emily sighed happily.

'Enjoying yourself?' asked Edgar, putting one hand on hers as it rested on the wooden rail.

Emily nodded, and did not remove her hand.

Emboldened, Edgar put his disengaged arm round the red coat.

'Emily – ' he began urgently, but Emily wriggled away.

'Oh, Edgar, don't spoil it!'

'What d'you mean – spoil it? I was only going to say, won't you come out with me again soon?'

Emily came to rest again, and looked down upon the Cax for a time before answering.

'I'd like to, Edgar, I really would. Only—'

'Only what?'

Emily turned to face him.

'Only this. I don't know if you take out lots of girls – but – well, I don't want to be one of a lot. That's all!'

Edgar laughed, and put his arm round her again. This time she did not wriggle away.

'Oh, Emily! You're a plain speaker, and no mistake. I can tell you truly – if you're willing to be my girl, then you won't have no others to worry about. You're the only one for me.'

'But, Edgar, don't say that! How d'you know how you'll feel in a month or so? We hardly know each other.'

'I know how I feel well enough,' said Edgar soberly.

'Well, I don't.'

'You'll get to know,' said Edgar comfortably. 'What about coming to the dance next week?'

'Thank you,' said Emily, in a small voice.

Edgar bent to kiss her cheek, but Emily, shying away, caused him to land a rather wet one on her brow.

They laughed together, and Emily moved away.

'Let's go back,' she said. 'We haven't tried the swing-boats yet.'

Together, hand in hand, they returned, like happy children, to the bustle of the market square.

Theirs had been an easy courtship, thought Edgar, looking back. There were no lovers' quarrels, no misunderstandings and no parental obstacles to overcome.

That auspicious Michaelmas Fair was in 1913, and throughout that winter and the following spring the young lovers were happy making plans for a wedding the following year.

'Better be October,' said Edgar practically. 'Have the harvest in nicely by then.'

'So I take second place after harvest!' quipped Emily, teasing him.

'As a farmer's wife, you always will,' replied Edgar. 'You know that without being told.'

Emily spent her evenings crocheting yards and yards of lace to edge tablecloths and towels. She still taught at Springbourne school during the day, and most of her earnings now went on linen for her bottom drawer.

Dolly Clare and Arnold Fletcher were also engaged, and the four friends had many outings together. Edgar grew less shy as their social circle widened, but there were one or two people whom he disliked and with them he had great difficulty in making conversation.

Dolly Clare's sister Ada was one of them. She and her husband Harry Roper ran a thriving greengrocery business in Caxley, and she invited the four to supper on several occasions.

There was a boldness about Ada which Edgar found highly distasteful. He hated boastfulness and pretence, and in the Ropers' establishment he found both in abundance. What Harry Roper called 'ambition' or 'getting on in the world', Edgar, with his solid country background, called 'doing down your neighbour', or 'cutting a dash'. Edgar felt fairly sure that Harry was not above using some doubtful methods of making a quick profit – all in the name of good business – and he did his best to avoid mixing with Ada and Harry.

Luckily, Emily was as distrustful of the two as Edgar himself.

'She was always top dog at home,' Emily told him, 'though Dolly's worth ten of her. She did some pretty mean things at school that I could tell you about, but won't. I never took to her.'

In the early summer of 1914, Ada's first baby was born, and Dolly was delighted to be godmother to John Francis.

It so happened that Emily and Edgar encountered Ada in Caxley one Saturday afternoon, pushing the baby in a very fashionable pram. Of course, they stopped to admire him.

The child was plump and pink, his dark head resting on a pale blue satin pillow decorated with lace and ribbons. He was asleep, and in his mouth was a dummy.

'Shall I take it out now he's asleep?' asked Emily, bending over the child. Ada gave her a cold glance.

'No, thank you. I can look after my own baby, I hope.'

'I'm sorry,' said Emily, discomfited. 'I know lots of babies use comforters, but our doctor told me that they can cause adenoids when the child's older. Lots of my children at school breathe through their mouths instead of their noses – and he says comforters may be the cause.'

'Maybe he's a busybody,' said Ada pointedly. 'I must be getting along.'

She swept away up Caxley High Street, and Edgar pulled a face at Emily.

'You copped it then,' he remarked. 'And you know, you did ask for it.'

'I don't care,' said Emily stubbornly. 'That baby didn't need it when he was asleep, and I don't mind betting he'll get adenoids, and probably protruding top teeth as well, if Ada lets him go on with it!'

It so happened that the years were to prove that Emily Davis was correct. Needless to say, it did not endear her to Ada Roper.

'The cheek of it,' she had said to Harry later that day. 'A

spinster like her – telling a mother what to do with her own child! I fairly froze her, I can tell you. Adenoids indeed! She and that doctor of hers want their heads seen to!'

Edgar and Emily were never invited to the Ropers' house again. They were not surprised – only mightily relieved.

They had been happy days old Edgar mused, leaning back in his wooden armchair and closing his eyes against the dazzle of the warm sunshine.

No one, least of all young lovers, bothered about the political happenings across the Channel. The course of the seasons rolled steadily onward. Ploughing, harrowing, drilling, planting – the long days in the fields and farmyard passed swiftly away, and their wedding day was only two or three months ahead. The two were as blithe as nesting birds, when the blow fell.

War with Germany was declared on August 4, 1914, and within a month Edgar was training in Dorset with other young men from the Caxley area. He and Arnold Fletcher had leave at the same time in November, and both came to Beech Green to see their girls. For Arnold, it was the last time, for he was killed by a hand-grenade thrown into his trench near the Ypres Canal, one cold and cruel February day in 1915.

The months which Edgar spent fighting in France were like a nightmare to him. Remembering them now, in the September sunlight, so many years later, they still seemed unbelievable.

The constant noise, the habitual grip of fear, the stench of rotting corpses, the rats, the sea of grey mud broken only by the stark splinters of shattered trees, were so alien to the young Edgar's home background of quiet green beauty that he was in a constant state of horror and shock.

Some men managed to keep up a stout heart, even addressing their dead comrades with cheerful badinage as they passed up and down the trenches. This ghastly bonhomie Edgar found callous and macabre. His gentle nature was crushed and appalled by the sights and sounds around him.

When the gas attacks finally caused his collapse, and he was invalided out of the army, he returned to England with a thankful heart.

A thankful heart, indeed, remembered old Edgar, stirring uncomfortably in his armchair, but a changed one too.

What went wrong with his love for Emily in those dreadful months that followed? To say that his war experience had unsettled him was to make the whole affair seem too slight and uncomplicated. But, nevertheless, that was the root of the matter.

Lying in his white bed at the Bournemouth hospital, he had gazed at the green trim lawns and the leafy trees, remembering his comrades in that grey, shattered landscape overseas.

On some days the English soil trembled with the thunder from the distant guns in France. Edgar rolled his aching head from side to side in sympathetic anguish.

It was as though his mind were split in two. One half was here, with his suffering body, in this quiet room with birds and flowers outside. The other half, writhing and tortured, still inhabited that nightmare world of dying men and hopelessness. Perhaps there was an element of guilt in poor Edgar's mind at this time. Other men were in danger. He was safe. But should it be so? He tortured himself with thoughts of Arnold Fletcher, and other young men who had been his friends at Beech Green, sharing his background, his work and his play – men who had ploughed, sown and threshed with him, batted and bowled on Beech Green's cricket pitch, shared his laughter and his hopes. Where were they now? And could he ever return, to face those who had loved them, seeing the sadness – and perhaps the resentment – in their eyes?

When Emily came on her weekly visits, the first flood of joy at her approach gradually ebbed away in the face of these secret fears. Outwardly, Edgar seemed calm, but Emily sensed that all was not well with him. There was a barrier now across the easy passage of their affection. She put it down to general physical weakness, and to the horrors which a sensitive spirit like Edgar's would find hard to overcome. She never doubted that all would be well in time.

Remembering that steadfast trust, old Edgar groaned aloud, and buried his face in his hands. He should have waited! He should have waited! All would have come right for them both if he had been patient – as patient as poor Emily was!

He rocked himself to and fro. To think that something which happened nigh on sixty years ago could still give such pain!

He remembered his terrible tears when Emily had gone each week to catch the last possible train back to Beech Green. It was not her going which upset him so dreadfully, but the knowledge that he would never be able to face life with her. For in his present state he never wanted to see Beech Green again, or those who lived there.

He wanted to run away from all that had happened, to start afresh, where no one knew him, where he could make a new beginning, leaving the pain and heartbreak behind.

The Irish nurse, Eileen, had comforted him during these outbursts. She was kind and motherly, it seemed to Edgar, ready to hold his hot head against the starched bib of her apron.

Later, he realised, she never spoke of Emily or his return to her.

In his weakness, he clung to her for support and advice. She gave both freely, never displaying the quick temper and sharp tongue which made her so heartily disliked by the other nurses.

In truth, Eileen Kennedy was looking for a husband, and in Edgar she thought she had found one who would suit her very well. She liked the idea of being a farmer's wife. She knew that Edgar would follow his father one day, and she enjoyed country life. Also, she was tired of nursing. She was twenty five and was determined to marry. The fact that Edgar was already engaged weighed with her not at all. Emily she considered a poor thing. Victory should be easy.

She conducted her side of the campaign with ruthless subtlety. Circumstances were on her side. She was with him constantly, and he was dependent on her for all his comforts. She was careful to keep out of Emily's way, when she paid her visits, so that her rival's suspicions were not aroused.

Edgar, weak in body and torn in spirit, gave way with little resistance. Eileen, as a young woman, had physical charms which faded after a few years of marriage, but in her nursing days she was trim and comely, with fair hair neatly waving under her flighty starched cap.

By the time Edgar's convalescence came, and he was moved a few miles away, there was a firm understanding between them. Now there was a dream-like quality, for Edgar, when Emily visited him. It was if she were a ghost from the past – that past he wanted so desperately to forget.

He was too weak to tell her about his plans. This cowardice was to colour his whole life. It haunted him whenever he was unable to sleep, in the long years which lay ahead. He never forgave himself.

Eileen encouraged him to keep silence.

'You aren't up to a scene,' she persuaded him. 'Write her a letter. You can put it all so much better in a letter.'

The little she had seen of Emily made her realise that she would accept the situation more readily with a letter before her. She recognised Emily's pride, and suspected rightly that she cared enough for Edgar to abide by his decision, no matter how cruel it might seem.

The scheme worked. Edgar was freed from his engagement, and he turned to a triumphant Eileen. Emily continued as best she could. No other man came into her life. For Emily, Edgar was her only love, both then and forever.

It was a week or two after his engagement to the nurse, that Edgar first had an inkling of her true nature.

He broached the subject of where they should live when he had quite recovered.

'Why, Beech Green, surely? You say there's a house there for you,' said Eileen briskly.

Edgar gazed at her in dismay.

'But you know how I feel about going back. I want to start somewhere quite new.'

'Who'd have you, except your father?' asked Eileen flatly.

'I expect I could get a job with another farmer,' began Edgar, much shaken.

'Another farmer would want a full day's work from you,' said Eileen. 'Your dad will let you go your own pace for a bit. And there's the house. It sounds just right for us.'

Edgar roused himself.

'But surely, you wouldn't want to go back there, where everyone knows about me and Emily. You'd feel uncomfortable.'

Eileen gave a hard laugh.

'It'd take more than Emily Davis and a parcel of gossipers to make me uncomfortable. She had her chance, and lost it. It's our life now, and we'd be fools to throw away a house and a job ready-made for you.'

'But, Eileen – ' protested Edgar, tears of weakness filling his eyes.

'No buts about it,' said Eileen ruthlessly. 'It's Beech Green for us, so get used to the idea.'

She whisked out of the room, leaving Edgar to his melancholy thoughts. For the first time, he began to realise that he had made a mistake, and one which was to cost him dear.

Old Edgar sighed, and reached for the last potato.

Humiliation, self-reproach, gnawing remorse and a lifetime of bitterness had been the result of a few vital months of

sheer cowardice. God knows he had paid heavily for his mistake! Worse still, he had made innocent, loving Emily suffer too. The encounter by the wood had told him clearly all that he had suspected – that Emily's love remained constant, and that his did too. It had been his lot to see the finest woman he had ever known tortured, year after year, on his account.

And now she had gone.

He bent his grizzled head over the last of his task, and a tear rolled down his cheek.

'What's up?' snapped his wife, appearing suddenly, throwing a shadow between him and the sunshine.

'Sun in my eyes,' lied Edgar.

But he knew that, for him, the sun would never be as dazzling again.

7 Ada Makes Plans

THE news of Emily's death spread rapidly when *The Caxley Chronicle* made its weekly appearance. Most readers turned fairly quickly, after reading the headlines, to the column headed 'Births, Marriages and Deaths', choosing the one of the three divisions most appealing to them, according to the age of the reader.

Ada Roper, widow of the prosperous greengrocer Harry, and sister of Dolly Clare, naturally looked first at the 'Deaths'. When one is in one's eighties there is a certain macabre pleasure in reading about those whom one has outlived.

She sat in her sunny drawing room on this shimmering September morning, a cup of coffee beside her, and a magnifying glass in her hand the better to read the small print.

The house, 'Harada', which Harry had built in the 'twenties, weathered the years well, and though her son John had once tried to persuade her to move to something smaller, Ada was resolute in her refusal.

'Why should I?'

'Because it's so expensive, for one thing. Fuel, rates, furnishings – and so much housework. I could easily find you a nice little flat – '

'I don't want a nice little flat. And anyway, I shan't need to buy any more furniture, and if I did move into a poky little place somewhere, what should I do with all these nice pieces your Dad and I collected over the years?'

'You could sell them,' suggested John.

'Never!' cried his mother. 'No, John. This is my home and I'm stopping here. I've quite enough money to see me out, thanks to the business, and with Alice to help me the work is very light.'

Alice was the companion who had come to live with Ada soon after Harry's death. She was a gentle soul, herself a widow, but a penniless one, and glad to have a comfortable home and pocket money in return for an amount of work which would have daunted many a younger woman.

John, seeing the position pretty clearly, was sensible enough to insist on plenty of reliable daily help. Alice, he knew, was worth her weight in gold as a companion. She was genuinely devoted to his mother and took her somewhat over-bearing ways with cheerful docility.

If she left, it would be impossible to find another person so amenable. John had no desire to have his mother living at his own house. His wife and children were positively opposed to the idea when he had once broached the subject tentatively.

'No fear!' said his wife flatly.

'Grandma? Live here? Oh no!' cried his children. And though he had upbraided them with their selfishness, secretly he was very relieved. If his mother was happy to squander her money on that great house, then he would see that things were arranged to keep her there in contentment. But, now and again, a little secret resentment clouded John's thoughts. What would there be left, when the old lady died, if she continued to live in this way?

John's good business head always ruled his heart, which is

why his parents' shop continued to thrive under his management.

At the time of Emily Davis's death he was a man in his late fifties with the dark florid good looks of his father.

A fine moustache and an expensive dental plate improved his looks as he grew older. As a young man, the slightly protruding top teeth had given him a rabbity look. Whether the comforter, abhorred by Emily, and the subsequent thumb-sucking had anything to do with it, one could not be sure. His mother, rather naturally, thought not. But Emily's words rankled for many years, nevertheless.

John took infinite pains with his clothes, going to London for his suits, which did not endear him to the local tailors. He presided over the shop in well-cut tweeds or worsteds, his dark hair carefully brushed, his expensive shoes as glossy as horse chestnuts.

His wife looked across the breakfast table, on this September morning, and thought how remarkably young he looked as he read *The Caxley Chronicle*.

'I see Aunt Dolly's Emily has gone,' he said, eyes fixed upon the paper.

'Poor old thing,' said his wife perfunctorily. 'But she must have been terribly old.'

'About the same age as mother, I should guess. They were at school together, I know.'

'What will happen to Aunt Dolly?'

John lowered the paper thoughtfully.

'I don't know. I really don't know.'

He rose, tugging at his jacket and smoothing his hair.

'She really shouldn't be alone there,' said his wife solicitously. 'Anything might happen.'

'I might drive over and see her,' said John, kissing her swiftly. 'It's rotten getting old. This'll cut up Aunt Dolly badly.'

During the day he turned over in his mind the possibilities for Dolly Clare.

Could she be persuaded, he wondered, to leave the Beech Green cottage and make her home at 'Harada'? There were points in favour of such a move.

For one thing, it would be further company for his mother, and if anything happened to Alice then Dolly, presumably, would still be there. It was another hedge against the possibility of his mother having to live in his own house some day.

Again, Dolly's little cottage, humble though it was, was exceedingly pretty, and just the sort of place which was being snapped up by Londoners looking for a weekend cottage. A similar one at Fairacre, John remembered with a glow of pleasure, fetched five thousand pounds last month. The money could be invested and add to Aunt Dolly's tiny pension, thought John solicitously.

Besides, it would be keeping the money in the family.

He spent much of the day working out little sums – the possible interest that Dolly Clare would get on her problematical gains, if invested wisely – and it was almost time to leave the shop before he faced the cold fact that Dolly might not wish to sell, and that his mother might prefer to have 'Harada' to herself.

He determined to go and see his mother that evening and to make a few delicate enquiries.

Meanwhile, Ada too had been thinking. This death of Emily created some problems. She was honest enough to admit to herself that she did not feel any grief on Emily's behalf. There had never been any love lost between the two.

Even now, Ada felt resentment at the way Emily had usurped her own place in young Dolly's affections. As little children in Caxley, Dolly had always followed Ada's lead. She adored her elder sister, and had been content to do her bidding without question.

But things had changed under the influence of the Davis family, and particularly with the growth of the friendship between Emily and Dolly. Now Ada was not always right. Dolly began to question some of her decisions, and to ask Emily's opinion before her sister's. Ada considered Emily a subversive influence, and, as she grew older, she found no reason to change her views.

Then there was the affair of Manny's marrow which had made young Emily a minor heroine. The boys' attention had been diverted from Ada, the queen of the playground at Beech Green School, and although it was only a temporary defection, it gave Ada further cause to dislike Emily.

Later still, when Ada was a young mother, and not long after the little contretemps of the baby's dummy, Emily played a more important part in Ada's life. It was an episode which she remembered with shame for the rest of her life, and Emily's attitude at the time did little to assuage Ada's guilt.

Even now, over half a century later, she shied away from the remembrance, although she knew from experience that it would return before long to haunt her. Did Emily ever tell? Did Dolly ever know?

The anxiety pricked her as keenly now as it had so many years ago. And she would never know the answers! Sometimes the old Jewish God of Retribution seemed very real to Ada.

The thought of Dolly brought more practical problems to her mind. She would be left alone in the little house at Beech Green, and would be worse off without Emily's financial help in the partnership they had so much enjoyed.

It was all very tiresome, thought Ada with exasperation. She supposed she ought to invite her to 'Harada'. It would be expected of her, by her local friends, she had no doubt, and when one was so well respected in the church, and particularly in the Mothers' Union, it behoved one to act correctly.

But why should she alter her comfortable way of life to accommodate a sister who really meant very little to her? They had gone their own ways for so long, that, despite a proper sisterly warmth when they met, they had little in common.

Would Dolly mix comfortably with the prosperous widows who still came occasionally to play bridge in Ada's drawing room? She was far more likely, thought Ada, to sit in a corner, like a death's head at a feast, while the chatter went on, making everyone self-conscious.

And how would Alice like it? After all, she must consider Alice's feelings. She might very well feel hurt at another person coming to live at the house, on intimate terms. And, of course, it would make more work. There would be another bed to cope with, more laundry, more heating in the bedroom, more vegetables to peel, more meat to buy. Really, the more one thought of it, the greater the problem became.

She was restless and irritable throughout the day, wondering what to do. She wanted to appear generous in the sight of the little world of Caxley, but she very much resented the discomfort and expense it might put her to.

So like Emily, she thought distractedly, to go first, and leave such a muddle for others to tidy up!

Perhaps John might be of help. She determined to telephone him, as soon as he returned from the shop. After all, Dolly was his godmother, as well as his aunt. He should give her some attention at this difficult time. It was all too much for Ada alone.

Really, she felt quite faint with worry about it. She went to the drawing room door and called Alice.

'Could we have tea early, dear? My poor head's throbbing. Jam and cream with the scones, Alice dear.'

But there was no need to make a telephone call, for John appeared very soon after the meal had been dispatched, and broached the painful subject with masculine frankness.

'Bad news about Emily Davis. You saw it, I expect, in the paper?'

'I don't know what's bad about dying in your eighties,' said Ada tartly. 'Surely it's only to be expected. I know I feel very near my end often enough.'

John sensed from this reply that his mother was in one of her difficult moods. The dash of self-pity in her last sentence was always a danger sign.

He patted her hand kindly.

'You're a wonderful old lady,' he assured her. 'Lots of happy years ahead for you.'

She allowed herself to be slightly mollified.

'Yes, well – I suppose I do keep pretty bright, considering. But it's always a shock when one of your own generation goes.'

'Aunt Dolly will miss her,' said John, approaching the subject of his schemes warily.

'Bound to,' agreed Ada. She brushed a scone crumb from

her lap and considered how best to put her difficulties to John.

'She shouldn't be alone,' said John. 'Not at her age.'

'No,' said Ada. 'Not at her age. And she's never been really robust. She was always the weakling of the two of us.'

'It's a problem.'

'It certainly is.'

'I take it she'll be pretty hard up?'

'No doubt about it. They shared expenses, of course, which helped them both.'

John stood up and balanced himself first on his toes and then on his heels. It was a habit he had had since childhood, and indicative of mental unrest. Ada found it irritating.

'Don't keep rocking, John.'

'Sorry, mother,' he said, standing stock still. 'It's just that I'm a bit worried about poor Aunt Dolly. She is my godmother, you know.'

'I know well enough,' snapped his mother, resenting the reproachful note in John's voice. 'And you're not the only one to be worried. I've been almost distracted, wondering what to do for the best, all day today.'

John felt that some progress was being made.

'What had you in mind?'

'Well, naturally, as she's my only sister, my first thought was to invite her here.'

'That's very generous of you, mother. But do you think you are up to it?'

Ada sighed heavily.

'We all have to make sacrifices at times like this. And no doubt Dolly would appreciate it.'

'I'm sure she would be most grateful.'

'But then – I don't know. It would be such a complete

change in her way of life, wouldn't it? And we're so far here from the shops and things. Have you considered having her at your house? She is your godmother, you know.'

John, though taken aback at this surprise attack, rallied well.

'Out of the question,' he replied swiftly. 'No spare room, for one thing, and then I think Aunt Dolly would find the children too much for her.'

'Humph!' snorted Ada, thwarted. A short silence ensued.

'If she *did* leave Beech Green, I think she would get a very good price for the cottage,' said John at last. His mother's love of money was as strong as his own. He could have found no surer way of diverting her attention.

'Would she now?' said his mother speculatively. 'How much should you think?'

'Somewhere in the region of five thousand.'

Ada nodded slowly.

'She'd need some of that to see her fixed comfortably for the rest of her life, of course – ' Her voice trailed away.

'Naturally, naturally,' agreed John hastily. 'Properly invested it should bring in a nice little sum for the next few years.'

He cleared his throat fussily.

'How old is dear Aunt Dolly now?' he asked in a would-be casual tone.

'Eighty-four,' said Ada shortly.

'She's made a will, I hope?'

'I believe so. I know if she went first, the house was to be Emily's.'

'Really?' John sounded startled. 'And now what happens?'

'I'm not sure, but I've an idea it might go to a niece of Emily's.'

It was John's turn to sigh.

'Ah well, she must do as she likes with her own property, of course, but I do hope she isn't making a mistake. Well, mother, how do you feel about inviting her here? Would you be happy about it?'

'I must think it over. I'm sure poor Dolly would enjoy the greater comfort she'd get here, and she'd have company, of course, but it would mean a lot of extra work. Not that I'd mind that – I've worked all my life – but I shouldn't like to place a burden on Alice.'

'Of course not,' agreed John. 'You think it over, my dear, and give me a ring, before you write to Aunt Dolly.'

He kissed her cheek and departed, leaving her to her thoughts.

* * *

Five thousand, thought Ada. It was worth keeping in the family. She reviewed the situation anew. There were arguments for and against inviting Dolly to 'Harada'. She pondered on the problem in the gathering dusk.

At last she came to a decision. She would write to Dolly expressing sympathy, and telling her that she could make her home in Caxley should she wish to do so. Then, in all truth, she could tell her friends that she had invited Dolly to live with her, and any money would be wisely invested for her maintenance. John would see to that.

She went to her writing desk and wrote swiftly in her large, bold hand.

Dear Dolly,

I was most distressed to hear about poor Emily and hasten to send my deepest sympathy.

You can guess how worried I am to know you are quite alone now. Should you care to come and stay here with me, you know you would be most welcome. For a short visit, if you prefer it, to see how you like it here, but with a view to living here permanently, I mean.

The back bedroom is very comfortable, although it is facing north, and the little box room next door could be turned into a snug little sitting room, if you like the idea.

I know you wouldn't want to be idle, and Alice and I would welcome your help in running the house.

Do think it over. I know John would be very happy to give you any help in disposing of your furniture and so on, if the need arises.

With love from,
Ada.

She glanced at the clock. If Alice hurried, she could catch the last outgoing post at the main office in the High Street.

She stuck on a stamp with an energetic banging, and called imperiously for Alice.

When she was safely dispatched on her hurried errand, Ada rang John to tell him what she had done.

He was a trifle annoyed that she had written without consulting him again, but he was resigned to his mother's high-handed and impetuous methods.

'Well, we'll have to wait and see now, won't we?' was all he found to say.

But as he put the receiver down, he had a strong feeling that Aunt Dolly's cottage would never be his.

He was right.

Two mornings later, he called to see his mother, who handed him Dolly's reply in silence.

My dear Ada,

Your kind sympathy is very much appreciated. I miss dear Emily more than I can say, as you may imagine, and because of that I am doubly grateful for your kind suggestion of sharing your home with me.

It is a very generous gesture, Ada dear, and I have thought about the matter seriously. However, I am determined to stay here, where I am so happy, and I am lucky enough to have good neighbours who will always help me, I know.

Perhaps John would bring you out to tea one day when things are more settled, and I can thank you both properly for all your concern for my welfare.

Your loving sister,
Dolly.

'That's that then,' said John, returning the letter. They both sighed. John for the loss of a dream; his mother with secret relief.

8 Did Emily Tell?

ADA'S relief was genuine. There would have been many drawbacks to Dolly's presence in the house. Perhaps the most irksome would have been the constant nagging query in her own mind: 'Did Dolly know?'

What was this guilty memory which worried Ada so unduly after so many years? And what part did Emily Davis play in it?

It was the age-old story of a boy and a girl, and it all began when Ada went, as a young girl, to live with her grandparents in Caxley.

She had a job in a flourishing draper's shop in the High Street, and her bright good looks and flirtatious ways brought many a young man into her department.

She had many admirers, and among them was the younger son of Septimus Howard, whose baker's shop stood in the market square.

Leslie Howard was dark, gay and a lady-killer. He worked hard with his father and brother Jim, and drove a smart baker's cart on the rounds outside Caxley. Leslie Howard was known well in the neighbourhood. He was a great favourite with the young of both sexes; a charmer who had inherited the dark looks of his gipsy mother.

The older generation, particularly those sober chapel-goers who respected his father Sep Howard, shook their heads over

Leslie's goings-on, and warned their daughters about trusting such a flighty-minded young man. If anything, this increased Leslie's fascination in their eyes.

It was not long before bold Ada caught Leslie's eye, and he took to meeting her as soon as the shop closed. Ada was careful to say nothing about the meetings to her aged grandparents, but, of course, in a town of Caxley's size, the word soon went round.

In the meantime, however, the two young people enjoyed each other's company. Sometimes, Leslie made an excuse to take the baker's cart out in the evening, on the pretext of a forgotten delivery. He would pick up Ada, waiting in a quiet lane, and they would spend a blissful few hours before returning.

They attended several local dances held in the Corn Exchange. They were both fine dancers, and grew accustomed to much open admiration on the floor.

It was on one of these occasions that Ada's quick temper betrayed her. Another market square family, the young Norths, were present at the dance. Bertie North had brought his younger sister Winifred, whose pale blue frock and silver ribbons were more splendid than any other gown to be seen at the dance.

Leslie turned his attentions to his old friend Winnie, and danced with her far more frequently than Ada thought suitable. It was true that kind-hearted Bertie had taken pity on her, but Ada, becoming crosser as the evening wore on, decided that Bertie was simply patronising her.

Her anger grew. The Norths were a prosperous family. The father, Bender North, had a thriving ironmongery business in the square, and Hilda North, his wife, could afford to dress well and to see her children beautifully clothed.

Ada considered the family 'stuck up.' In those days of class consciousness, she felt that the Norths were above her. The Howards were poorer, and with Leslie she felt comfortable. Bertie's good clothes and gentle manners made Ada feel rebellious and discomfited.

It was the beginning of the end of the affair between Leslie and Ada, but although they rarely met after the dance, there was a strong personal bond between them. They both possessed outstanding vitality, and the attraction they felt for each other did not grow less by being pushed underground.

Ada heard of his subsequent marriage to Winnie North with secret envy, although by that time she too was married to Harry Roper, and was the mother of a baby son.

Leslie came into Ada's life again during the 1914-1918 war. She met him, quite by chance, one bright October evening as she walked along the tow path by the gently flowing Cax.

Baby John was safely in bed, looked after by a little maid-of-all-work who lived over the shop with Ada. Harry was serving in Italy, and from his boisterous letters seemed to be happy in the army.

Ada was bored and lonely. She worked hard in the shop all day, but when she had locked its door, and she had shared a meal with the little maid and kissed young John 'Goodnight', she took a brisk walk before darkness fell. Partly she felt the need for exercise and fresh air, but even more strongly she needed to pass away the long hours of evening time.

In war-time in Caxley, there were very few social occasions. With the young men gone, there were no dances or socials – nothing to give Ada the stimulus she loved.

She had a wardrobe packed with pretty clothes, for Harry was a generous husband, but no occasion to wear them. There were long ankle-length gowns trimmed with lace insertion and rows of diminutive buttons. There were smart fitted coats with fur at the hem and frogging across the front. There were several muffs to match the coats; and in a separate cupboard stood a dozen or more beautiful hats, some trimmed with feathers, or laden with silken flowers, or edged with fur or swansdown. Perched above Ada's bright gold hair, well-skewered with hat pins for safety, they crowned Ada's beauty with added glory. She mourned the fact that in war-time there were so few times when she could dazzle Caxley with such finery.

She met Leslie face to face as she took her walk along the tow-path, and her heart leapt at the sight of him. He looked even more dashing than usual in uniform.

He held out both hands, and she put hers into them. They stood looking at each other, without speaking for a full minute.

Beside them the Cax gurgled. A few leaves fluttered down upon its silky surface and were borne away. The dry reeds whispered as the slow current moved them, and nearby a moorhen piped to its mate.

'Ada,' said Leslie, at last, very low, 'I've been longing to see you again.'

'I've missed you,' replied Ada simply.

She turned to walk beside him. It was as though no rift had ever occurred between them. In that one short minute, they were once again in complete accord.

'I've ten days leave,' said Leslie, matching his step to hers. 'Can I see you again?'

'I usually come here for a walk about this time,' said Ada.

Neither said a word about wife or husband. There were no

enquiries about their respective families, no polite small talk about the town or general matters.

Both knew instinctively that the feeling between them was too strong to be denied, and time was short. To be in the presence of the other was all that mattered.

For the next few days, Ada lived in a state of feverish excitement which she found difficult to conceal. She met Leslie each evening, sometimes by the Cax, sometimes in a quiet lane where prying eyes would not see them.

Leslie's leave ended at the weekend, and he persuaded Ada, with very little difficulty, to go away with him on the Saturday before he reported to his unit on the Sunday night.

'But Winnie?' said Ada, speaking at last of his young wife.

'She thinks I have to be back on Saturday. We can go to Bournemouth. No one knows us there. I know a decent hotel.'

Ada's heart leapt. Here was excitement, a change from stuffy Caxley and the dreary round of keeping the shop going. The thought of the neglected gowns in the wardrobe, now to see the light of day again, made her eyes sparkle.

Leslie kissed her swiftly.

'We can go on the morning train, travelling separately until we change at the junction, in case there are any old codgers who might tell tales.'

They laughed together. They were like two children, plotting mischief. To neither of them occurred the possibility of wrong-doing or disloyalty to their partners. They were perfectly matched in selfishness and animal vitality.

The plan worked smoothly. Ada left little John with his doting grandparents, on the pretext that an ageing aunt of Harry's wanted to see her in Sussex, and she felt that she must make the journey for Harry's sake.

As arranged, Ada made her way to the head of the platform, assiduously avoiding looking at the further end where a soldierly figure waited, his eyes, apparently, gazing down the line.

Leslie had made his farewells to Winnie at home, begging her not to upset herself by saying farewell in public. Winnie, touched by his thoughtfulness, had agreed to his plan.

The train arrived in a flurry of steam and smoke. Doors banged, porters shouted, the guard blew his whistle shrilly and waved his flag.

At that moment, a small figure hurtled from the booking office, wrenched open the nearest third-class door, and leapt inside.

Emily Davis had caught the train by the skin of her teeth yet again.

She was on her weekly pilgrimage to see Edgar in hospital at Bournemouth. At this time, she was acting headmistress at the little school at Springbourne, for her headmaster was in the army, and as it happened, was fated never to go back to Springbourne. On his safe return at the war's end, he moved to a larger school, and Emily continued as headmistress in her own right.

Running the school while he was away in the army was a heavy task for Emily, but one which she tackled with her customary energy. The hardest part was the journey back and forth each weekend to see poor Edgar.

His progress was so pathetically slow. The gas attacks had affected his lungs, and a painful cough persisted. He seemed to live for the week-ends, and Emily travelled on Saturday morning and returned on the last train on Sunday.

This meant that all her domestic work had to be fitted in during the evenings or very early on Saturday morning. The school house at Springbourne was small, but inconvenient. Water had to be wound up from a well in the garden. The bath was a zinc one which hung at the side of the garden shed, and had to be carried into the kitchen, there to be filled from hot saucepans and kettles bubbling on the kitchen range.

Emptying the bath was almost as great a labour as filling it.

Emily overcame all these difficulties effortlessly. After all, this was the way in which she had been brought up as one of a large and cheerful family. But she wished, sometimes, that Edgar were nearer, for the journey was tedious and involved precious money as well as precious time.

On this particular morning, she changed as usual at the junction, and whilst she was collecting her hand luggage together, she saw Ada, exquisitely wrapped in a fur-trimmed coat, with a hat and muff to match, moving swiftly towards a waiting figure. They linked arms and, heads together, made their way to the waiting train.

Emily recognised Leslie Howard. It was plain from their behaviour that they were completely engrossed in each other.

Emily hung back out of sight, and quickly climbed into an empty carriage at some distance from the couple. She did not want to embarrass them, and she also needed to mark some tests of the children's which she had brought with her in her bag.

But as she put the ticks and crosses automatically against the answers, Emily's bewildered brain tried to take in the full import of this meeting.

At Bournemouth she waited until the couple had gone

through the barrier, and then gave in her ticket and made her way straight to the hospital.

Edgar's eyes lit up when he saw her walking down the ward. She kissed him gently and let him tell her all his hospital news – what the doctor said that morning, what meals they had been given, the excitement of a visiting soprano who had made their heads ache with patriotic songs.

Emily gave him the Springbourne news and the little presents of farm butter, brown eggs and late roses from his family. But she said nothing of Ada and Leslie.

She stayed nearby in a shabby house which supplied bed and breakfast for a small sum. The woman was kind, but too busy to take much interest in her lodgers. There was nowhere to sit, and Emily was accustomed to walking along the promenade or looking at the windows of the shut shops on Sunday morning, until it was time to visit Edgar again.

This Sunday morning was clear and sunny. The sea air was heady, the sea-gulls cut white zig-zags across the blue sky, screaming the while. Emily gulped down the salty air, revelling in the fresh breeze on her face. A bright October day had a flavour all its own. Here, by the sparkling sea, everything was extra sharp and beautiful.

She went at a brisk pace, but presently slowed up. In front of her strolled Ada and Leslie. His arm was round her waist. Her head was almost upon his shoulder. They might have been a honeymoon couple. Passers-by looked at them fondly and with some sympathy. So many young men in uniform came here for their leave, and many of them never returned to England again. Let them enjoy life, said their indulgent smiles, while they can!

Emily was about to turn round and escape when, to her

horror, they turned too. She was conscious of Ada's eyes upon her – eyes which widened in surprise. Emily bolted toward the rail of the promenade and, leaning over, gazed out to sea. She did not dare to move for a full five minutes.

When at last she turned, she saw the pair far away in the distance. They were as lovingly entwined as ever.

Emily made her way thoughtfully to see Edgar.

Ada was perturbed by the encounter.

'That was Emily Davis,' she told Leslie when they were out of earshot.

'And who's she?'

'Dolly's friend. Teaches at Springbourne.'

'I don't believe it,' said Leslie stoutly. 'You're getting fanciful.'

'I'd know that ghastly old hat of hers anywhere,' replied Ada, tossing her own furry beauty proudly.

'What does it matter anyway?'

'Supposing she tells somebody?'

'She won't. Why should she? It's none of her business what we do.'

'She doesn't like me. She might feel like making mischief.'

'Rubbish!' cried Leslie. He stopped by the end of a shelter, where they were hidden from sight, and took Ada in his arms. His kisses were not returned as ardently as before.

'Ada! Don't let this silly business upset you.'

'I bet she tells Dolly anyway,' said Ada spitefully. 'They never keep anything from each other.'

'Forget it,' said Leslie, drawing her close. She struggled free.

'It's all right for you. You're going away. I've got to go back and face them all. Suppose Harry gets to hear of it?'

'And suppose he doesn't!'

'Or Winnie?'

'They won't! Come back to the hotel and calm down.'

He guided his love back to the privacy of the hotel, and there they stayed, very happily, until it was time for Ada to catch the train home.

Emily, of course, had to catch the same train. She was careful to get into it early, and to busy herself with her books.

There was no sign of the couple and she began to think that they must be staying in Bournemouth when, at the last moment, they hurried on to the platform.

Ada climbed into a carriage only two from Emily's. There was little time for farewells for the train was about to move off, but Ada leant from the window and clung passionately to Leslie's neck for a brief moment, crying his name.

The train chuffed off, leaving Leslie, hand upraised, on the platform. Emily heard the window pulled up with a bang, and before she had time to wonder if she could slip down the corridor to a carriage further away, Ada herself appeared in the corridor.

She stopped dead, her chest heaving beneath its smart frogging, and tears still wet on her cheeks. She cast a look of venom upon poor Emily, who gazed back transfixed, as an innocent rabbit might when hypnotised by a stoat.

Ada turned and re-entered her compartment. Emily, sorely troubled, did her best to read a paper by the meagre light afforded by war-time illuminations.

At Caxley Station they reached the ticket-collector side by side.

Ada thrust her ticket into his hand and spoke in a vicious whisper to Emily.

'You keep your mouth shut,' she hissed.

She never forgot the look which Emily gave her from those clear grey eyes.

Emily said no word, but the look expressed loathing and contempt. In that moment, Ada was forced to face the truth that little Emily Davis, poor, shabbily dressed, a humble inky-fingered school-teacher was her peer in all that really mattered. There was no disguising the fact that Emily had every right to despise her.

When, in later times Ada looked back upon that mad weekend, which was never repeated, she realised that it was that look of Emily's which brought home to her the wickedness and cruelty of her behaviour.

It was the first step towards Ada's heart-searching, and her first true encounter with the feeling of guilt.

And now Emily Davis was dead, thought Ada, the old woman. She had kept silence. She had carried Ada's secret to the grave with her. Of that, Ada had no doubt. She would have heard soon enough, in Caxley, if Emily had ever breathed a word.

There had been many moments of panic for Ada in the years that followed. Harry was a loving and generous husband, but he would never have forgiven infidelity, Ada knew well. She trembled when she thought how completely she was at the mercy of Emily Davis. It made her dislike of Emily stronger than ever, for now it was allied to guilty fear.

Yet, in her heart, she felt sure that her secret was safe. That look which Emily had given her at Caxley Station expressed not only contempt, but also her own shining goodness. Emily Davis would not stoop to anything as shabby as tale-telling.

The old lady sighed, and picking up the poker, stirred the fire.

'Well, at least she made me take a look at myself,' she said aloud.

'Who, dear?' asked Alice from the other side of the hearth. She lowered her knitting and looked in bewilderment at her employer.

'Emily Davis. She made me look at myself. What's more, she made me see plenty to dislike when I looked.'

Alice studied the wrinkled face with some concern. For the first time, she saw humility written there.

9 Jane Draper at Springbourne

AMONG those who read the brief notice of Emily's death in *The Caxley Chronicle* was Jane Bentley, who had started her teaching career, many years before, under Emily's guidance at Springbourne School.

She was now a woman in her late fifties and lived in a village to the south of Caxley, some fifteen miles from Springbourne. She had not kept in touch with her old headmistress, but occasionally they had met by chance in Caxley, and were always glad to see each other.

As a child, Jane Bentley, then Jane Draper, was delicate, the type of child who spends a large part of the winter in bed, the prey of every epidemic in season.

Luckily, she was intelligent and fond of books. The youngest of four, she became an aunt in her teens and had plenty of experience with children. She decided to become an infants' teacher.

The Draper family lived in a respectable London suburb. Money was short, but with wisdom and thrift the family managed adequately. It was a sacrifice to let Jane go to the training college of her choice, for although she received a grant, and a loan which had to be repaid in the first three years of teaching, in the normal way she would have been earning at the age of eighteen, and able to augment the family income.

She was a conscientious girl doing well at college and, honouring her pledge to return to the authority which had financed her, she started her teaching career, in the bleak early thirties when posts were so scarce, at a large infants' school in her native borough.

She found the work tough going. Nervous and apprehensive, she discovered that she was expected to teach a class of fifty six-year-olds to read, to write, and to imbibe the rudiments of arithmetic. These three Rs in some form or other, and with a break for physical training, made up the morning's time-table. The afternoons were given over to such infant delights designated as Art, Music, Handwork, Free Expression, and the like.

Her headmistress was a forceful woman, over endowed with thyroid and the relentless energy which goes with it. She did her best to be patient with the succession of young teachers who passed through her hands, but it was plain that their slowness and lack of class discipline, allied to some vague and high-faluting clouds of Child Psychology which they trailed behind them from college lectures, drove the poor woman to distraction.

Miss Jolly – for that was her unlikely name – came into Jane's classroom one day to see what all the hubbub was about. She found Jane sitting at her table with half a dozen children round her, holding reading books. One of the books was upside down.

The rest of the class seemed to be wandering restlessly about the room, some children holding pieces of equipment, some gazing through the window at another class in the playground and others enjoying themselves by sweeping their fellow pupils' work from the tables with happy cries.

'What are they doing?' asked Miss Jolly in a voice of thunder.

'They're Working At Their Own Pace,' replied Jane, rising to look over the heads clustered about her.

'Half of them aren't working at all,' rejoined Miss Jolly truthfully. 'Get them to their desks.'

Poor Jane did her best by clapping her hands ineffectually and crying, in a voice faint with nervousness, for order. A few, who had noticed Miss Jolly's presence, had the good sense to obey, and sat, smiling smugly, at the chaos around them.

For almost two minutes, agonisingly long to Jane Draper, she did her best to make herself heard. At last Miss Jolly came to her aid.

'SIT DOWN!' commanded that lady, in tones which set the windows vibrating. Children scurried to their chairs.

'HANDS IN LAPS!' ordered Miss Jolly. They obeyed to a man. Even Jane's particular problem child, Jimmy Lobb, who had frequent fits – some of them quite genuine – subsided into his chair and sat mute and wide-eyed. They knew the voice of authority well enough, and most of them unconsciously welcomed it.

'You are making far too much noise,' Miss Jolly told them sternly. 'How can Miss Draper hear this group read?'

Rightly, the subdued class assumed that this was a rhetorical question and remained suitably mute.

'Has everyone got work to do?' asked Miss Jolly.

'Yes, Miss,' came the meek reply.

'Very well. You get on with it, and you STAY IN YOUR DESKS until the clock says half-past.'

She pointed to the enormous electric time-piece on the wall which jerked the minutes along in staccato fashion.

'When that big hand gets to 6,' she continued, improving

the shining hour, 'you may CREEP from your desks to change your apparatus. NOT BEFORE! You understand?'

'Yes, Miss,' came the dulcet whispers.

'Those who were reading come quietly to Miss Draper's table,' ordered Miss Jolly. 'And I want to see every book the right way up.'

A demure half-dozen tip-toed politely to their former positions. Jane found the whole exercise unnerving, and hoped that Miss Jolly would soon leave her to her usual muddle.

But for a full five minutes, Miss Jolly prowled about the room, whilst work went on in an unnatural hush. Jane found herself trembling with anxiety.

At last, Miss Jolly departed, requesting Jane to meet her in her room as soon as school dinner was over.

By the time the meeting took place, Jane was in a state of panic. She entered the well-polished room, blind to the Della Robbia plaques, the cut-glass vase of roses, the silver desk-calendar (a parting gift from another school) and the hand-tufted rug on the floor.

Miss Jolly was kind but firm. She began by praising Jane's conscientious approach to teaching, her punctuality, her neat Record Book of Work to be done weekly, and did her best to put the dithering girl at ease.

She did not succeed, for in Jane's bewildered brain the phrase 'Damning with faint praise' beat about inside her head like an imprisoned bird, as she tried to listen to Miss Jolly's controlled commendations.

'You see,' said Miss Jolly at last, approaching the heart of the matter. 'We set ourselves certain aims in this infant school – aims of *attainment*, I mean. Ideally, each child should go forward to the junior school able to read – the most important thing – to write, and with a working knowledge of the four rules, at least in tens and units, preferably with hundreds too. Then, of course, they should have some idea of common measurements, be able to tell the time – '

'But there are *so many* of them!' wailed poor Jane.

'Unfortunate, I know, but there it is. What you have to learn, my dear, is to get them to do as they are told WHEN they are told. You saw what happened this morning.'

'But they really *were* working,' protested Jane. 'They must move about to fetch the next piece of apparatus. It shows they are keen to get on when they get one card done quickly and hurry out for the next.'

'It could show that they are bored with the piece of work in front of them,' said Miss Jolly. 'As far as I could see, quite a number of them couldn't be bothered to finish one job before trying their luck with the next. It's no good letting them get slack. You must check their progress. The bright ones will get on whatever happens. It's the idle ones who need prodding.'

'But if they're *interested*,' began Jane, 'they'll *want* to work. At college – '

Miss Jolly, with one eye on the clock, and patience sorely tried, let herself be told about Self-Determination, A Child's Natural Thirst for Discovery, and Working At One's Own Pace.

'Yes, well – ,' she said, when Jane had come to a faltering halt. 'Don't forget that a very small percentage are paragons. The rest, like most of humanity, are bone idle.'

Jane, horrified by such heresy, was about to argue, but Miss Jolly raised the capable right hand which had slapped so many infant legs.

'Keep the aims in mind, my dear. We want to send these children along to the junior school well equipped. If you can get the results by the methods shown you at college, well and good. But they won't work unless you have control of the class. Without that, nothing will work.'

She rose, and Jane made her way to the door.

'You're doing very well,' said Miss Jolly kindly. 'I think I shall be able to give you a good report at the end of this probationary year.'

'Thank you,' said Jane huskily. 'If only there weren't so many in a class, I think I'd manage better.'

'Wouldn't we all?' said Miss Jolly, with feeling. She gazed speculatively at Jane for a moment, and spoke again.

'I could offer you *forty backward* children next year, if you like the idea. Think it over, dear. Think it over!'

Jane did think it over. She thought a great deal in that first gruelling year, and many a time she despaired of continuing in the career she had adopted.

Would she ever become a fully-certificated teacher at the end of this probationary year? Did she want to be one for the rest of her life? And what could she do, if she wanted to change her job?

There were plenty of long queues outside the Labour Exchanges. Some of her college contemporaries were on the dole. It was a dispiriting situation.

She was not sure that Miss Jolly was right in her attitude to the children. She seemed to be far more concerned with the school's record of achievement than with the children themselves. Jane felt that she demanded too much of them, and of her staff. Not all of them were possessed of the self-assurance and drive which had swept Miss Jolly into a headship at a relatively early age.

On the other hand, she had the sense to realise that Miss Jolly did not ask anything of her teachers which she could not do herself. She might not conduct a class as Jane's college lecturers had recommended, but she certainly got results, and the children seemed to thrive. It was all very confusing.

At the end of the year, she was relieved to know that her work had been considered satisfactory. She was asked again if she would take the 'small' class of forty backward children, and agreed.

And so it came about that one September morning she faced her new class. Most of the six-year-olds were backward because of absence from school through illness. Some were mentally unsound and a few of these children would become certifiable at the right age. Some were incorrigibly lazy and would always lag behind, and a few were rebels by nature against any sort of discipline and authority, and likely to remain so for the rest of their lives.

Jane grew very fond of them. For one thing, they were grateful for any effort made for them. They were wildly delighted with such simple creations as a paper windmill or a lop-sided blotter, and carried these treasures home with far more care than their more brightly endowed fellows. They were affectionate and anxious to please. Jane found their goodwill exceedingly touching.

She also found them exceedingly exhausting, and returned home each evening tired to death. She had no heart for any sort of social life. Early bed was the thing she craved most, and her mother grew alarmed.

The family doctor prescribed iron tablets and sea-air. The

iron tablets were taken regularly and seemed to do some good. Sea-air was more difficult to come by. The family had no car, and money was still short.

When, in February, Jane was forced to take to her bed with influenza and was unable to leave it for three weeks, the doctor spoke his mind to Mrs Draper.

'That girl of yours upstairs,' he told her frankly, 'is wearing herself out. She's no reserves of strength at all. See she gets a holiday by the sea, after this, and then a teaching post that's easier than this one. Don't you know any school that has small classes?'

The Drapers did not. But during the summer term, when Jane was back at school and still struggling feebly with her forty backward children, a post was advertised in *The Teachers' World* for an assistant mistress to take charge of eighteen infants at Springbourne School.

'Number on roll,' said the advertisement, 'forty-eight.'

A whole school, with only forty-eight, thought Jane longingly!

She looked up the village in the ordnance survey map. It was, she saw, a few miles from Caxley where one of her college friends lived.

She wrote to her, and asked for her advice and for any information.

'Come and see it for yourself,' was the answer, and with a glow of hope Jane went to spend the weekend with the Bentleys.

They were a happy-go-lucky family living on the northern outskirts of Caxley, some three miles from Springbourne. To reach the village the two girls cycled along a quiet valley beside a little river full of water-cress beds. It ambled along sedately beneath its overhanging willows on its way to join the Cax.

It was a Saturday morning, warm and sunny. The school, of course, was uninhabited and so was the school house, for Emily had gone on the weekly bus to do some shopping in Caxley.

Emboldened, the two girls pressed their noses to the classroom windows and gazed at the interior. To Jane it seemed like a dolls' school after the enormous building in which she taught. She caught a glimpse of a large photograph of Queen Mary as a young woman, wasp-waisted in flowing white lace, with pearls in her hair.

The desks were long and old-fashioned, housing five or six children in a row. But there was nothing old-fashioned about the stack of new readers on the piano – Jane was using the same series herself – and she noted, with approval, the children's large paintings, the mustard and cress growing in a shallow dish, and the goldfish disporting themselves in a roomy glass tank, properly equipped with aquatic plants.

The playground was large, and shaded by several fine old trees. Elder bushes, turning their creamy flowers to the sun, screened the little outhouses which were the lavatories.

It all seemed cheerful and decent, a kindly spot where one could be happy, and could work without heart-break.

When Jane returned, she applied for the post and was accepted. Later that summer she met her headmistress-to-be for the first time.

She was in the playground carrying a tear-stained five-year-old in her arms. She kissed it swiftly before putting it down,

and advanced to meet Jane. It gave Jane quite a shock. Would Miss Jolly do that?

'I'm so glad you can come and help us next term,' said Emily Davis, holding out her hand.

And, as Jane held the small warm brown one in her own, she felt that, at last, she had come home.

10 The Flight of Billy Dove

THERE began then for Jane a period of great happiness and refreshment which was to colour her whole life.

To begin with, she stayed with the hospitable Bentleys, for the first few weeks of the autumn term, until she could find suitable lodgings nearer the school. After so much ill-health and strain, it was wonderful to be taken into the heart of such a cheerful family, and Jane thrived.

The bicycle ride to school and back brought colour to her cheeks, and an increased appetite. In those first few weeks of mellow autumn sunshine, Jane began to realise the loveliness of the countryside.

Harvest was in full swing, and the berries in the hedges were beginning to glow with colour. The cottage gardens were bright with Michaelmas daisies and dahlias, and the children brought sprays of blackberries and early nuts for the classroom nature table. Sometimes Jane received fresh-picked field mushrooms which the children had found on the way to school, or a perfect late rose from someone's garden.

She revelled in the bracing air of the downs and, encouraged by her headmistress, took the infants' class for nature walks round and about the village.

She found the children amenable and friendly. They might lack the sharp precocity of her former town pupils, but their slower pace suited Jane perfectly. Facing a class of eighteen, after forty or fifty, was wonderful to the girl. There was so little noise that there was no need to raise her voice. She could hear each child read daily – a basic aim she had never been able to achieve before – and found the children's progress marvellously heartening.

Of course there were snags. The chief one was the range of ages. The youngest was not yet five; the oldest – and most backward – nearly eight. But Jane was used to working with groups, and found that discipline was no bother with so few children who were mostly of a docile nature. Relaxed and absorbed, Jane's confidence in her own abilities grew steadily, and she became a very sound teacher indeed.

Emily Davis played her part in this process. Jane found her as quick and energetic as Miss Jolly had been, but with a warmth of heart and gentleness, both lacking in her former headmistress.

Emily was like a little bird, Jane thought, with her bright eyes and brisk bustling movements. The children loved her, but knew better than to provoke her. They knew, too, that a cane reposed at the back of the map cupboard. No one could remember it being used, but the bigger boys, who occasionally assumed some bravado, were aware that Miss Davis was quite capable of exerting her powers, if need be, and kept their behaviour within limits.

Emily's high spirits were the stimulus which these children needed. Mostly the sons and daughters of farm labourers, they were unbookish and inclined to be apathetic.

'Don't forget,' said Emily to Jane one playtime, as they sipped their tea, 'that most of them are short of food, and quite a number go cold in the winter. Times are hard for farmers and their men.'

'But they look well enough,' observed Jane.

'Their cheeks are pink,' answered Emily. 'If you live on the downs you soon get weather-beaten. And by the end of the summer they are nicely tanned. But look at their bodies when they strip for physical training! You'll see plenty of rib cages in evidence. There's just as much poverty in the country as in towns. The only thing is it's not quite so dramatic, and fewer people see its results.'

There were such families at Springbourne, Jane soon discovered. She saw too how Emily coped practically with the situation, supplying mugs of milky cocoa during the winter to those who needed it most. Those who did not run home for their midday meal brought sandwiches, for this was before the coming of school dinners. One family, in particular, was particularly under-nourished. When the greasy papers were unwrapped, they were usually found to contain only bread with a scraping of margarine.

Many a time Jane saw Emily adding a piece of cheese to this unpalatable fare, and apples from her store shed. It was all done briskly, without sentiment, and in a way which would not make a child uncomfortable.

It was small wonder, Jane thought, that Emily Davis got on well with the parents. There were exceptions, of course, and one incident Jane remembered for years.

It happened just before Christmas one year. Emily had arranged a school outing to a Christmas pantomime, put on by amateurs, in Caxley. A bus was hired, and the fare and the entrance fee together would cost five shillings. Parents could join the party, and there was a good response, despite the fact that five shillings seemed a great deal of money to find just before Christmas.

The fact that several Thrift Clubs would be paying out about that time may have accounted for the enthusiasm with which Emily's venture was received. The money came in briskly until only young Willie Amey's contribution, and his mother's, were outstanding.

The day before the outing, Mrs Amey appeared, in tears. Asking Jane to keep an eye on both classes, Emily took the weeping woman over to the school house and heard the sad tale.

'That beast of a husband,' Emily told Jane later, 'took the ten shillings from the jug on the top shelf of the dresser, where she'd hidden it – or *thought* she had, poor soul – and drank the lot at the pub last night.'

'What will happen?'

'I shall put in the money for them,' said Emily shortly, 'and I'll see Dick Amey myself. He'll pay up, never fear!'

Jane gazed at Emily in trepidation. Dick Amey, she knew, was a big, burly, beery fifteen-stoner. Jane was afraid of him under normal circumstances. Provoked, he could be dangerous, she felt sure.

'But he's such a great *bully* of a man,' said Jane tremulously.

'And like most bullies,' said Emily forthrightly, 'he's a great coward too. I shall square up to him tonight.'

She went about her duties as blithely as ever that afternoon, but Jane was the prey of anxiety. She said goodbye to her diminutive headmistress that afternoon, wondering if she would see her unscathed next morning.

She need not have worried. Evidently Emily had put on her coat and hat as soon as she thought Dick was home, and had climbed the stile, crossed a field to his distant cottage, and tapped briskly at his door.

His frightened wife stood well back while the proceedings took place.

Emily had come straight to the point. Direct attack was always Emily's motto, and she got under Dick Amey's guard immediately.

'About as mean a trick as I've ever heard of,' said Emily heartily. 'But the money's in for both of them and they're going to enjoy the show. That's ten shillings you owe me. I'll take it now.'

Dick Amey, flabbergasted, demurred.

'I ain't got above two shillun on me,' protested Dick.

Emily held out her hand in silence. His wife watched in amazement as he rooted, muttering the while, in his trouser pocket and slammed a florin into the waiting palm.

'When do I get the rest?' said Emily.

'You tell me,' growled Dick.

Emily did.

'A shilling a week at least, till it's done,' said Emily. 'You keep off the beer for the next few weeks and you'll soon be out of my debt.'

Jane heard of this memorable encounter from Mrs Amey herself, long after the event. It must have looked like a wren challenging an eagle, thought Jane. But, no doubt about it, the wren was the victor that time.

* * *

Jane found permanent accommodation in a tiny cottage on Jesse Miller's farm at Springbourne.

It had been empty for some time, but was in good repair, for the Millers were always careful of their property.

It consisted of a living room and kitchen, with two small

bedrooms above. The place was partly furnished and Jane had the pleasure of buying one or two extra pieces to increase her comfort. The rent was five shillings weekly, and the understanding was that if Jesse Miller needed it for a farm worker sometime, then there would be a month's notice to quit.

She was now a near neighbour of Emily's, and frequently spent an evening with her headmistress and old Mrs Davis who now lived with her. Emily's father had died some years before and it had taken much persuasion to get her mother to leave the family cottage at Beech Green where she had reared her large family. But at last she consented, and had settled very well with Emily.

The two had much in common. They were both small, energetic and merry. Jane found them gay company, and often looked back, in later years, upon those cheerful evenings when the lamp was lit and stood dead centre on the red serge tablecloth, bobble-edged, which Mrs Davis had brought from her old home.

They knitted, or worked at a tufted wool rug, and chattered nineteen to the dozen. The schoolhouse living room had an old-fashioned kitchen range with a barred fire and two generous hobs on which a saucepan of soup, or a steaming kettle, kept hot. It was all very snug, and Jane was always reluctant to leave the circle of lamp light to make her way home along the dark lane, following the wavering pool of dim light from her torch.

Often, she went to Caxley to see the Bentleys, for Richard Bentley, an older brother of her college friend, became increasingly attentive. He owned a little car and worked in a Caxley bank.

As the months passed, he came to fetch Jane from the cottage more and more frequently. When they became engaged, Emily Davis was the first to hear the news.

She was genuinely delighted, though not surprised, and kissed young Jane soundly.

'And don't have a long engagement,' urged Emily.

'But we must save some money,' protested Jane, laughing at her vehemence.

'Don't wait too long. I did, and I lost him.'

Her face clouded momentarily and, for the first time, Jane realised that this cheerful little middle-aged woman must once have been young and in love, and then terribly wounded.

It was the first she had heard of the affair, although she learnt more later.

'I'm sorry,' she said, taking the older woman's hand impulsively. 'I had no idea.'

'Well, it's over and done with,' said Emily, with a sigh. 'But take my advice. Marry soon.'

The two planned to marry in the spring of the next year, and at Easter 1939, Jane was married from her parents' house in London.

After the honeymoon, they settled at the Springbourne cottage, intending to move nearer Caxley when something suitable came on the market. Jane had resigned her teaching post, but still saw a great deal of Emily and her pupils.

When war broke out in September of that year, young Richard Bentley, who was in the Territorial Army, went off to fight.

Jane resumed her job as infant teacher at Springbourne School, and went to Caxley Station, with her headmistress, to collect forty or so evacuee schoolchildren who were to share Springbourne school for the duration of hostilities.

The war years had a dream-like quality for Jane Bentley. At times, it was more of a nightmare than a dream, but always there was this pervading feeling of unreality.

Had there ever been such a golden September, she wondered, as that first month of the war?

Day after day dawned cloudless and warm. Thistledown floated in the soft breezes. Butterflies, drunk with nectar, clung bemused to the buddleia flowers, or opened and shut their wings in tranced indolence upon the early Michaelmas daisies.

It was impossible to realise that just across the English Channel terror and violence held sway. At Springbourne one might have been swathed in a golden cocoon as the harvest was gathered and the downs shimmered in the heat haze.

Of course, at Springbourne School there was unusual activity as the newcomers settled down, amicably enough, with their native hosts.

Two teachers had accompanied the evacuees, one young, one middle-aged.

The middle-aged headmistress was a tough stringy individual with a voice as rough as a nutmeg scraper. She had run a Girl Guides troop for years, played hockey for her county and had the unsubtle team-spirit approach to life of a hearty adolescent.

She was billeted with Emily in the school house, and the two got on pretty well, both appreciating the other's honesty and concern for their charges. Miss Farrer, Emily discovered, was a whirlwind of a teacher, and a strict disciplinarian.

The younger woman, Miss Knight, was a different kettle of

fish altogether, and poor Jane, whose spare bedroom she occupied, suffered grievously.

Molly Knight was one who thrived on emotion. She travelled from one dramatic crisis to another as a traveller in a desert moves from oasis to oasis. If the war could not supply enough material for sensation – and at that stage it was remarkably dull – Molly Knight created excitement from the little world about her. She was a mischief-maker, mainly because of this desire for sensation, and Jane found her particularly exhausting.

'What can I do?' she asked Emily one day, in despair. 'I try to look upon it as my contribution to the war effort, but I really can't face Molly breaking into my room at midnight to tell me how atrociously the Germans are treating their prisoners, and giving me a blow-by-blow account of her reactions to some stupid piece of propaganda.'

'I've been thinking about it,' replied Emily. 'If Miss Farrer's willing, I suggest they have your cottage, and you come here. How do you think that would work?'

Jane, despite a certain reluctance to leave the cottage, fell in with this plan, and for some time the two establishments were thus constituted. It made things easier in every way.

As the phoney war, as it came to be called, continued, a number of the children and their parents returned to London. One who did not, much to Emily's and Jane's pleasure, was a particularly attractive eight-year-old called Billy Dove.

He was a red-haired freckled boy, quick and intelligent. There was no doubt in Emily's mind that he would go on to a grammar school in time.

He was the only child of a quiet little mouse of a woman, and the two were billeted in a cottage not far from the school.

The father was in the Navy, patrolling off the coast of Ireland, it was believed.

Mother and son were devoted. Mrs Dove was a great knitter, and young Billy's superb collection of jerseys was much admired. She did not mix much with the other women, although Billy was popular with the other children, frequently organising their games.

One day in late November the tragedy occurred. By now the weather had broken, and all day the wind had howled round Springbourne School and rain had lashed the windows. Playtime was passed indoors, in a flurry of well-worn comics on the desks among the milk bottles.

By afternoon, a fierce gale was blowing, ferocious enough to satisfy even Molly Knight's passion for excitement.

'Just look at the postman!' she exclaimed to Jane, as they watched the weather through the rain-spattered window. 'He can hardly walk against it!'

They watched him struggle up the path to Billy Dove's door, letter in hand. Water streamed from his black oilskin cape, and every step sent drops flying from his wellington boots.

The children were sent home at the right time, through the murky fury of the storm, with strict orders 'not to loiter'. Emily and Jane returned to the school house for tea, looking forward to a peaceful evening by the fire.

But at eight o'clock, an agitated neighbour arrived to say that Mrs Dove was in a dead faint across her table, with her wrists dripping blood, and that young Billy was nowhere to be found.

'You go and ring the doctor,' said Emily to Jane, 'while I run along to Mrs Dove.' They flung on their coats and hurried away on their errands.

The scene at Mrs Dove's, though frightening enough, was not quite as horrifying as the neighbour's breathless description had led Emily to believe.

There was blood upon the tablecloth, on the floor, and upon Mrs Dove's hand-knitted jumper, but the slashed wrists dripped no longer for, luckily, the poor woman's attempt at suicide had been unsuccessful. Emily had snatched up her mother's smelling salts on her way out, and now waved the pungent bottle before the pale face.

The neighbour found some rum in the cupboard, and when, at last, Mrs Dove came to, she and Emily made her sip a little rum and hot water.

'What ever made you do it?' asked the neighbour, bewildered.

Emily shook her head. This was no time to torture Mrs Dove with whys and wherefores. They must bide their time.

Although conscious, the woman said nothing, but sat, head sunk upon the bloodied jumper, in silence.

But when the doctor arrived, she stirred and pointed to a letter which had fallen to the floor. He read it, and passed it to Emily, without speaking.

It was a brief communication – that which Jane and Molly had seen the postman delivering that afternoon. It said that James Alan Dove was missing presumed killed.

'I'd like to have her in hospital overnight,' said the doctor. 'She's lost a good deal of blood, and is in a severe state of shock.'

'I understand,' said Emily. 'The boy is missing. I'll ring the police and start searching myself. He can stay the night at the school house when we find him.'

'By far the best thing,' agreed the doctor. If only more

women were like Emily Davis, he thought, turning to his patient!

The memory of that night stayed with Jane Bentley for the rest of her life. The two of them set out through the storm with only the faintest glimmer from torches, dimmed by tissue paper over the glass in accordance with black-out regulations, to guide them.

'We'll stick together,' said Emily. 'And keep shouting his name. Not that we stand much chance of being heard in this wind.'

'Which way?' asked Jane, at Mrs Dove's gate.

'Towards Caxley. He may have had some muddled idea of catching a train. Anyway, he wouldn't make for the downs in this weather. There's not a shred of shelter there.'

They splashed along the valley lane, past the school. The water gurgled on each side of the road, sometimes fanning across the full width where the surface tilted. Above their heads the wind roared in the branches, clashing them together and scattering twigs and leaves below. The elephantine grey trunks of the beech trees were streaked with rivulets of rain-water.

Jane's shoes squelched at every step. She could feel the water between her toes, and wished she had had Emily's foresight and had thrust her feet into wellington boots.

The little headmistress kept up a brisk pace. Every now and again she stopped, and the two would cry:

'Billy! Billy Dove! Billy!'

But their voices were drowned in the turmoil about them, and Jane began to wonder if the whole venture would have to be abandoned.

She followed in Emily's wake envying the older woman's unflagging energy.

'Are you aiming at anywhere particular?' she shouted above the din. Emily nodded.

'Bennett's barn and the chicken houses,' she responded. Jane knew that these buildings were Edgar Bennett's – that same Edgar, so she had recently learnt – who had jilted the indomitable little woman before her, so many years ago.

They splashed onward. Now the lane ran close by the little river. The watercress was now large and coarse, and swept this way and that by the torrent of water rushing through it. Who would have thought that the pretty summer trickle of brook, overhung with willows and long grasses, could become such a snarling leaping force, carrying all before it!

Emily turned left, and struck uphill along a rough track now streaming with chalky water from the downs. Some hundred yards up the hill, she left the track and beat her way, head down against the onslaught of rain, towards two large hen houses standing side by side in the field. Jane followed doggedly.

'Stand round here. There's more shelter,' said Emily. 'I'll only open the door a crack, otherwise the hens will be out. They're kittle-cattle.'

It was the first time Jane had heard this phrase. She savoured it now, watching Emily's small hand fumbling with the wooden catch of the door.

'Billy! Billy Dove!' she called through the chink. A pencil of light from the dimmed torch searched every cranny of the house.

There were a few squawks of alarm from the hens, and a

preliminary rumbling from the rooster before taking suitable action against those who disturbed his rest. But there was no human voice to be heard.

'No luck,' said Emily, shutting the door, and squelching across the grass to the next.

They were just as unlucky here.

'We'll try the barn,' said Emily, tucking wet strands of hair under her sodden head scarf. 'Back to the road, Jane.'

Jane found herself stumbling along, almost in a state of collapse. She was not as strong in constitution as Emily, and this evening's tragedy had taken its toll. She longed for bed, for warmth, for shelter from the cruel buffeting of the weather, and for the relief of finding the missing child.

She did not have to wait long. At the barn door, Emily motioned her forward. Together they moved inside, out of the wind and rain. It was quiet in here, and fragrant with the summer smell of hay.

Emily pushed aside the wet tissue paper from the torch, and a stronger light came to rest on a dark bundle curled up in an outsize nest in one corner of the barn.

Emily knelt down beside the sleeping child. His eyes were tightly shut, his red hair dark with moisture and clinging to his forehead. The cheeks were blotched and his eyelids swollen with crying. But he was unharmed.

'Billy,' whispered Emily. The child woke, and sat up abruptly. There was no preliminary stretching or yawning. Billy Dove was awake in an instant, and remembered all that had brought him to this place in blind panic. Emily knew how it would be.

'Mummy?' he asked, turning anxious eyes upon Emily. She took one of his grimy hands in hers.

'She's well again,' she told him. 'The doctor is looking after her.'

'And Daddy?'

'No one knows yet.' She gripped his hand more tightly. Obviously, the child had read the letter and understood his mother's action when he had found her slumped across the table.

'But what do *you* think?' said Billy, his bottom lip quivering piteously.

Jane, the silent spectator, never forgot Emily's reply, or the expression on her wet face as she made it.

'I think it would be wrong and wicked to stop hoping,' said Emily straightly.

The child sighed and struggled to his feet. Emily brushed the wisps of hay from his raincoat.

'You're coming to sleep in my house now,' Emily told him.

He managed a watery smile.

'Thank you, Miss Davis,' he said politely, holding open the door for her.

Jane Bentley put down *The Caxley Chronicle* slowly. Over thirty years had passed and yet she could remember that dimly-lit scene in every detail.

And now Emily Davis was dead!

Or was she, wondered Jane? What was that saying about those who lived in the hearts of others? Something to the effect that they never really died. If that were the case, then Emily Davis would certainly live on.

She herself owed much to Emily. She had gone to Springbourne a nervous, delicate girl with little to look forward to in the career which she had chosen.

Emily had given her strength and encouragement. She had sent her out into the healthy downland to regain her youthful spirits. She had taken in this apprehensive stranger and turned her into a happy confident member of the Springbourne family.

Whilst she was with Emily she had found health, happiness and a husband.

And more than that, she had found, by Emily's example, a way of living and a strength of character, both of which were to remain as guide-lines for the rest of her life.

Little Emily Davis's influence must have spread far, thought Jane, gazing into the September sunshine. Just as a small pebble, dropped into a still pool, spreads ever-widening ripples, so must Emily's impact have travelled through all the friends and pupils she had encountered.

What became of Billy Dove, she wondered? He certainly fulfilled the promise Emily foretold, and went on to Caxley Grammar School, then to a university, and was doing something quite important connected with mining, Jane believed.

There had been a happy ending to Billy Dove's war-time experience, Jane remembered, for his father had been picked up from the sea by a German ship and he spent the rest of the war, tediously but safely, as a prisoner. Billy's eyes had been like stars when he told Miss Davis the news, months after that never-to-be-forgotten night of storm and horror.

Dear Billy Dove, thought Jane, bestirring herself! He ought to know the news, but it wasn't likely that he took *The Caxley Chronicle* these days. He probably read *The Financial Times*, now that he was a prosperous man of nearly forty. No doubt he had done well for himself, but no doubt he often thought of Springbourne School and how much he owed to the guiding spirit who ruled it so wisely when he was young.

And in that, thought Jane Bentley, he would not be alone.

11 Billy Dove Goes Further

JANE BENTLEY was wrong.

Billy Dove read *The Caxley Chronicle* as well as *The Financial Times*. It arrived regularly each week, in a wrapper neatly addressed by his mother, wherever he might be in the wide world. The issue carrying the notice of Emily's death came to him in Scotland.

When his father, Petty Officer Dove, returned from prison camp at the end of the war, he found that his old London employer had died and the firm was no more. In a way, he was relieved.

He had had plenty of time for thinking in camp, and more and more his thoughts turned to the English countryside where he had been brought up. Now he longed to return.

After leaving the village school, he had been bound apprentice, at the age of fourteen, to a family firm of cabinet-makers in London. He lodged with an obliging aunt in Mitcham, worked hard, and gained steady promotion with the firm as the years passed.

In one of the terraced houses opposite his aunt's home, he found his future wife, a pretty little auburn-haired girl, who caught the same train into the City as he did to work as a copy-typist in an insurance firm.

They married when he was twenty-five and she was twenty-three, and made their home in a tiny flat two streets away from their former abodes.

Jim Dove often thought of those early married days, as he went about his tasks in the German prisoner-of-war camp. They had been happy enough, for they were young and very much in love. Young Billy arrived within the year, and was an added joy – a good-tempered, healthy baby, with his mother's red hair and his father's cheerful disposition.

It was now that the Doves began to long for more room. Their flat was on the first floor. Their landlady lived below, a hard-bitten widow who resented the necessity of letting part of her home.

Billy's pram was left in her tiny hall with her grudging consent. Billy's napkins and other family washing were allowed to blow on a two-yard line near the garden rubbish heap, screened from sight by a large golden privet bush. Except for the purpose of hanging out the washing, the Dove family was not allowed in the garden.

Peggy Dove bore the restrictions patiently. Times were hard, and she knew that it would be several years before they could hope to move to a house of their own. Meanwhile, she took Billy to the nearby park for his daily outing, and did her best to keep on good terms with the landlady.

Jim Dove fretted far more. When war came, and settled their future for them willy-nilly, he was relieved to know that his wife and son would be settled safely at Springbourne. He knew the Caxley area fairly well, for he and his father had been great cyclists, and had camped many a time on the banks of the Cax, and had pushed their bicycles up the steep flanks of the downs nearby. At sea, and later in the prison camp, he had found comfort in the thought of Peggy and Billy enjoying the countryside he knew so well.

He was determined that he would not return to London to live. It was no place for a boy to be brought up. Who knows? There might be more children, and a flat in London was little better than the prison he now inhabited, he told himself. He was tired of being cramped and confined. When he got back he would find a job in the country.

But would he? That was the problem. Would any other firm employ him? Peggy, cautious as a mouse, would tremble at the thought of any risk. She would try to persuade him to return to the old life, he felt sure.

Ah well! No use fretting about it whilst in German hands. He'd face that problem when the time came, Jim decided.

As so often happens, the problems resolved themselves by the time he was reunited with Peggy and Billy. The old firm had gone. Billy was now doing well at Caxley Grammar School, and Peggy had found a little cottage to rent on the edge of commonland within walking distance of Caxley. She wouldn't go back to London for a thousand pounds!

Jim found a post with a local firm of furniture makers, and the Doves settled down to make their life afresh. Jim and Peggy were destined to spend the rest of their long lives in Caxley, and to find contentment there.

Billy remained an only child, and a highly satisfactory one. He was almost thirteen when his father returned, and working well at the grammar school. He had found the transition from the little school at Springbourne to the large boys' school somewhat unnerving, but by the time his father came back he had settled down and was enjoying the work.

Eventually, he gained a place at Cambridge, obtained a good

class Honours degree, and became a mining engineer. His work took him all over the world, but at the time of Emily Davis's death he was in Scotland with his wife and two children. His assignment there was for approximately two years, and the Doves had rented a house for that time. It stood among pine forests, on the edge of a sizeable village where the children attended the local school.

The job was an interesting one. On the site of a long disused coal mine, other mineral deposits had been discovered, but at a depth and angle which made them difficult to work. It was Billy Dove's job to overcome the problem.

He had been chosen expressly for it by his firm because he had done so well on a similar project for the Italian government. On the slopes of Mount Etna in Sicily, certain minerals had been discovered in the volcanic rock which were of great interest to the chemical industry. The deposits were at a considerable depth, in one particular stratum formed by lava ejected some hundreds of years earlier. Billy found the work arduous but fascinating.

He was at work there for six weeks, and there was a possibility of returning for a further month when the drilling had reached the second stage. It was a prospect which he viewed with mixed feelings. For, to his mingled delight and guilt, sensible, steady Billy Dove, devoted husband and father, regular church-goer and wise counsellor to those asking his advice, had fallen head over heels in love with a girl in Sicily.

It came about like this.

Billy's firm had booked a room for him at a modest but respectable hotel in Taormina, a few miles from the working site.

He lost his heart to the little town at once. Perched on the sunny hillside, tall cypresses towering like dark candles above the freshly-painted houses, the place had unique charm. It was at the end of April when he saw it first, and the public gardens, laid out in broad terraces, were fragrant with wallflowers, pinks and stocks. The orange trees added the warm scent of their blossom and the beauty of their golden fruit to the scene. Wistaria hung in swags from the pergolas, and, in the sheltered garden of the hotel next door, sweet peas were already in flower.

In all his wanderings, Billy Dove had never yet discovered a place which enchanted him so swiftly and so completely. He gazed at the vivid green-blue sea far below, at the craggy mountain which overhung the town, and at Etna against the blue sky forming a majestic backcloth to it all.

In his spare time he explored the town thoroughly. The ruined Greek theatre fascinated him, and the view from its heights across the Straits of Messina to the distant mainland of Italy was one which never failed to thrill him.

He enjoyed plunging down the steep steps from one level of Taormina to the next. He sampled all manner of places to eat and drink, from tiny cafés, murky with smoke and crowded with noisy Sicilians, to cosmopolitan hotels offering the accepted variety of French cooking found in every tourist centre.

It was not long before he entered the San Domenico Hotel. It had once been a monastery, and about its ancient courts and stairways still clung the gentle silence of earlier days. Here Billy Dove found hushed peace and rare beauty. He also found unexpected, and shattering, love.

* * *

Emily Davis

The girl was small and golden. When Billy saw her first, she was clad in a brief white frock which contrasted with her glowing sun-tanned skin.

She was climbing up the steep slope from the swimming pool, carrying the bulky paraphernalia of an afternoon spent swimming and sun-bathing. Billy stood aside to let her pass, and the towel which was flung over one shoulder slid to the ground. Billy bent to retrieve it.

'Thank you,' said the girl, holding out a hand. Immediately, a Penguin book and one sandal clattered to the path.

The girl laughed as Billy bent again.

'I'm so sorry. It's like one of those circus acts, isn't it? You know, the clown drops one thing after another and then turns out to be an expert juggler.'

'And are you?'

'Does it look like it?' replied the girl. Her teeth were very white and even. Her eyes were a peculiarly light hazel which gave them a sunny look.

'Let me take some of the things,' offered Billy, genuinely concerned by the untidy collection of articles in her arms. 'Couldn't we put the small stuff in your bag?'

He squatted down and packed the book, two sandals, a spectacle case and a tube of skin-cream into the enormous beach bag. He then stood up and folded the towel neatly.

'You take that, and I'll bring the bag,' said Billy.

'No, really. I can manage perfectly now that you've tidied me up. You were going down to the pool, I expect.'

'I wasn't really going anywhere. Just savouring a perfect evening.'

More people began to descend the path, and Billy and the girl found themselves in the way.

'Well, thank you,' she said, moving on. 'I was going to have a drink before dinner. May I offer you one after all this porterage?'

'I should love it,' said Billy truthfully, following her nimble figure up the slope.

Over the drinks they introduced themselves and Billy told her about the work which brought him to Sicily.

'And you are on holiday, I expect,' he said.

'I have been. That's why I'm staying at the San Domenico. But I've come to a tremendous decision in the past fortnight. I'm hoping to settle here for good.'

'In this hotel?'

'Heavens, no! I should soon be broke. No, I've found a little house, higher up the hill. I've rented it for six months to see if life in Taormina is all I hope it will be. I've been looking for somewhere to settle ever since my father died last year.'

It appeared that her father had been a prosperous manufacturer in Yorkshire until a stroke had finished all activity for him. Mary had left her job as almoner in the local hospital to nurse him. Her mother had been dead for some years.

On her father's death she found that everything had been left to her. He was 'a warm man', as they said locally, but a large house on the windswept moors, despite two old-fashioned hard-working maids to help in running it, was not what Mary wanted.

She was over thirty now, and longed to get away. Too long, she felt, she had been mewed up in the old home. She craved for sunshine and change.

She left the house in the maids' care while she set about her restless wanderings. Almost a year was spent in this way, and now she longed for a home, and somewhere to settle, as urgently as she had yearned for flight. In Taormina she believed she had found her goal.

'If I find it to my liking,' she told Billy, twirling her glass thoughtfully, 'I shall sell the Yorkshire place and stay here permanently. I've nothing to take me back – no relatives, no ties of any sort—'

Her voice trailed away, and she looked directly at Billy.

'Are you staying for dinner?'

'I ought to go back to do some work.'

'Do stay,' she said impulsively. 'It's lovely to talk to someone again, and you've been so very kind.'

Of course he stayed. And every minute that passed made her company dearer to him. He promised to come and inspect the little house on the morrow, and to help in any way he could with the move.

Billy Dove walked home, through the moonlit scented night, tingling with the most unusual sensations.

'My God!' said Billy, addressing a stone dragon on a gate-post, 'it's love again!'

In the days that followed, Billy felt himself the battleground of conflicting emotions, and very exhausting he found it. He had been a fairly uncomplicated character for almost forty years, distrusting violent emotion, and impatient with those who seemed to have no control of their feelings. He had met many philanderers in his travels, and had a hearty dislike of them. Those who boasted of their conquests he found doubly boring. They did not impress Billy Dove.

'Time you grew up,' he would tell them, yawning, and walk away.

And here he was, behaving in exactly the same way. The guilt he felt when he thought of his disloyalty to Sarah and the boys was overwhelming, but only momentarily so. It was swept away by this new wave of fierce, youthful, exulting happiness. Before its onslaught he was powerless.

Mary's passion matched his own. It was as though, with so little time before them, their love had an added urgency. They spent every possible hour together, turning their minds away from the inexorable advance of the day of Billy's departure, like children who hide their eyes from a wounding light.

Taormina, and the golden girl, were heartrendingly beautiful when that last day came.

'You'll come back? Say you'll come back!' pleaded Mary, clinging to him.

'You know I can't promise that,' said Billy. She knew about Sarah and their two children, and he had been careful not to raise her hopes by telling her of the possibility of further work on the site. Cruel though it seemed, they must make the break.

He flew from Catania that morning and he saw the green and golden island tipping beneath him. He changed planes at Rome, and found he had to wait for three hours. He spent the time pacing restlessly up and down in the windy sunshine, his mind in turmoil.

He flew from Catania that morning and he saw the green and golden island tipping beneath him through a blur of tears. He changed planes at Rome, and found he had to wait for three hours. He spent the time pacing restlessly up and down in the windy sunshine, his mind in turmoil.

By the time he arrived at Heathrow, in pouring rain, he was calm enough to have made two decisions. This sweet mad interlude was over, and he would not see Mary again. Secondly, Sarah must never know anything about it.

12 The Return of Billy Dove

IT is easy enough to make good resolutions. Keeping them is another kettle of fish.

The decision to keep his guilty secret from Sarah was comparatively simple. He was deeply ashamed of his behaviour, although the remembrance of those few idyllic weeks would never fade, and would colour the rest of his life.

Billy was not the sort of man to unload his guilt on to another. What good would confession do to Sarah? No, he owed it to her to keep silent, and by his extra care of her, and the boys, to salve his smarting conscience.

But the decision to make a clean break with Mary was seriously undermined when a letter arrived from his firm asking him to return to the Sicilian site for the second stage of the work. Could he let them know how the Scottish project was moving? At a pinch, young Bannister could take over one or the other while he was away. He would need thorough briefing, of course, and it was to be hoped that Dove could arrange to carry on with both jobs. What did he feel?

What did he feel, echoed Billy! He put the letter to the side of his breakfast plate, and gazed out at the wooded Scottish hillside. In the garden John and Michael raced round and round pursued by a floppy-eared puppy. There were his two fine boys, full of roaring high spirits. He must do nothing to hurt them.

He looked across the table to Sarah, immersed in *The Caxley Chronicle* which had arrived with the morning letters. She looked very young and defenceless, despite her thirty-odd years, in her blue and white cotton frock. A little frown of concentration furrowed her smooth brow.

'There's an Emily Davis in the "Deaths",' she remarked. 'Could it be your old teacher?'

'I should have thought she'd died years ago,' remarked Billy absently, his mind on his problem.

'Well, she was eighty-four,' said Sarah, her eyes still fixed on the paper. 'Died at Beech Green. Might well be, don't you think?'

She looked up. Billy was standing at the window, gazing into the garden. It was apparent that he had not heard her remarks. She was accustomed to his complete withdrawal from the world around him when his mind was perplexed, and was not unduly upset.

'Heavens, it's late!' she cried. She ran to the open window and called to the boys.

Billy shook his head, as though he had just emerged from deep water. He put his arms round her swiftly and kissed her with sudden fierceness.

Sarah laughed.

'Don't dally, darling,' she said, 'or the boys will be late for school.'

Within two minutes, the three were in the Land-Rover waving goodbye to Sarah at the window.

The road was steep, and wound its way downhill between dark fir woods which Billy found beautiful on a sunny morning, but sinister and silent at other times. Nothing grew beneath their shade, and Billy often thought longingly of the oak and hazel woods of his childhood at Caxley, starred in spring with primroses and anemones, and gay with the golden tassels of catkins.

The village school stood back from the road with a wide green verge before it. As Billy drew up, the bell was clanging from the little bell-tower, and the children were already forming lines ready to lead in. The two boys gave him hasty wet kisses, scrambled down, and raced to join their fellows. The schoolmaster was a stickler for punctuality.

He waited to see them take their places in the lines. John turned towards him and gave an enormous wink of triumph, as if to say: 'Done it!', just as the lanky form of the headmaster appeared at the school door.

Amused, Billy drove off slowly. There was a lot to be said for a village school education when one was eight, robust and cheerful.

He had been eight, he remembered sharply, when he was at Beech Green Village School. But, though he may have been robust, he had been far from cheerful at that time.

What would he have done without Emily Davis just then? At the same age as John, frightened and horror-struck, he had been rescued by her efforts. He had never forgotten that night of storm and terror.

And she was dead? Is that what Sarah said this morning? Eighty-four, and at Beech Green? He mused as he wound his way towards work. That would be Emily Davis, without doubt.

He sighed deeply. She was a grand old girl! His thoughts strayed from the events of that wild night to another phase of his school life when, as a bewildered eleven-year-old, Emily Davis had come, once more, to the rescue.

* * *

The transition from the tiny world of Springbourne to the comparatively large one of Caxley upset the boy more than he would admit.

Instead of racing the few yards along the village street from his home to the school, he now had to rise much earlier and catch a bus into the town. His comfortable hand-knitted jerseys and flannel shorts, now gave way to a grey flannel suit with long trousers. Black laced shoes, polished overnight, took the place of easy well-worn sandals, and on his head he wore the familiar Caxley Grammar school cap, with much pride, but some irritation – for wasn't it just one more thing to take care of, and to remember to bring home at night?

At times, young Billy felt burdened with all these belongings. They weighed as heavily upon him as the shining new leather satchel which bumped against his hip as he walked.

He was bewildered too by the sheer size of his new school and by the hundreds of boys. When you have been one of forty or fifty children at school assembly, and one among only twenty or so in the classroom, it is unnerving to be cast among four hundred-odd boys, all larger than oneself.

To Billy, some of the prefects were men. Certainly, some of them looked quite as mature as some of the young masters. They filled the boy with awe with their tasselled caps, their gruff voices and their sheer size when they passed him in the corridors.

The standard of work, too, presented a problem. At Springbourne School he had held his own with little effort. Now he was among boys brighter than himself. There were new subjects to tackle, such as French, Latin and Algebra. At times, sitting at the cottage table, with his homework books spread out in the light of the Aladdin lamp, he came near to despair. Would his mind ever be able to hold all this mass of new knowledge?

But it was the affair of the conkers which brought all his troubles to a head. Billy had always loved the glossy beauties which tumbled from the Springbourne trees in the autumn gales. He collected them with the eye of a connoisseur, and Billy Dove was recognised by the other boys as a champion in the conker-playing field.

He owned a metal meat skewer which bored a hole beautifully. Only Billy's closest friends were allowed to borrow it. He was equally particular about the type of string he used to thread his collection. All in all, Billy Dove brought the care and use of conkers to a fine art.

He was delighted to find a stout horse-chestnut tree on the way from Caxley station to the school, and he filled his new jacket pockets with some splendid specimens. At playtime (which he tried, in vain, to remember to call 'break' now), he turned out his collection on the grass of the school field and, squatting down, began to sort them out for size. His metal skewer was in his inner pocket with his new fountain pen and propelling pencil. He produced it, ready for action.

At that moment, a shadow fell across him, and looking up he saw one of the prefects who was on duty.

'Whose are these?' said he disparagingly.

'Mine,' said Billy, blinking against the sunlight.

'Stand up when you talk to me.'

Billy obeyed briskly.

'What are these for?' continued the lofty one.

'To play with.'

'To play with,' mimicked the older boy. 'You'd better learn

pretty smartly that we don't play kids' games like conkers here. Chuck them away.'

'But why—?' began Billy rebelliously.

'Don't argue. Throw them in the dustbin. And pronto!'

'Can't I take them home?'

The prefect took hold of Billy's left ear, and twisted it neatly.

'You talk too much, young feller. Do as you're told or I'll report you. And pick up every one. Understood? If they get in the school mower old Taffy'll murder you.'

His eye lit upon the skewer.

'And I'll confiscate that. Dangerous weapon, that is. You can ask for it back at the end of term.'

There was nothing for it but to obey. Furious at heart, Billy collected the shining conkers, grieving over the satin skins so soon to wither in the dustbin.

The prefect accompanied Billy to the dustbin and watched him deposit his treasures. He tossed the skewer nonchalantly from hand to hand as the disposal of the conkers went on.

Billy made one last bid for his property.

'If I promise to leave my skewer at home, can I have it back?'

The prefect stood stock-still, his eyes narrowing menacingly.

'Don't you understand the King's English? You'll get it back – IF you ever get it back – at the end of term. Clear off, and think yourself lucky not to be reported for disobedience!'

A dangerous weapon, thought Billy murderously, watching his enemy depart. That's what he'd called his beloved skewer. At that moment, in Billy's hands, it might well have been an instrument of fierce revenge.

This happened on a Friday. He returned home, moody and pale-faced, his satchel heavier than ever with weekend homework, and his heart heavier still. His mother was wise enough to refrain from questioning, but she watched anxiously as the boy fiddled about with his exercise books at the table, obviously unable to concentrate.

He slammed them together eventually, and spent the rest of the evening slumped in a chair with a library book. There was still a good deal of work to be done, his mother knew. Usually, Billy tried to get the major part of it polished off before the weekend began, but it was plain that he was in no mood to tackle it tonight.

He was little better next morning, and his mother sent him to the village shop for some goods. It was there that he met Miss Davis, also armed with a basket. Her quick glance noted the heavy eyes and unusually sulky mouth.

'How's school?' she asked amiably.

'All right,' said Billy perfunctorily.

'Lots of prep?'

'Too much. Much too much.'

Billy sighed. Miss Davis felt a pang of pity.

'Have you got time to help me saw some logs this afternoon?'

Billy's face brightened.

'Yes. I'd like to. What time?'

'Any time after two. Ask your mother if she can spare you for a couple of hours. I'd be glad of a hand.'

She packed her basket neatly, smiled at Billy, and departed. Cheered at the prospect of some physical activity, Billy set about his shopping in better spirits.

Clad in his comfortable old jersey and shorts, Billy reported for work at a quarter past two. Emily was already hard at it, at the end of the garden, saw in hand.

'My poor old apple tree,' she told him, pointing the saw at

the fallen monster. 'It's been rocking for two or three years, and last week's gale heeled it over.'

'We'll never get through the trunk with these saws,' observed Billy.

'No need to. It's just the branches we'll have to do. A man's coping with the main part next weekend.'

They applied themselves zealously to the smaller branches. Billy found the work wonderfully exhilarating. The smell of the sawn wood was refreshing, and a light breeze kept him cool.

He enjoyed stacking the logs in Emily's tumble-down shed, and made a tidy job of it. The rough bark, grey-green with lichen, was pleasant to handle, and his spirits rose as the stack grew higher and higher.

'It will probably be enough for the whole winter,' he said,

sniffing happily. Emily straightened up and, hands on hips, looked at their handiwork with satisfaction.

'Easily, Billy.'

She gave a swift glance at the boy, now flushed and panting with his exertions.

'Have you had enough, or shall we finish the job?'

'Let's finish,' said Billy decidedly.

They worked on in companionable silence. Sawdust blew across the grass, as the saws bit rhythmically through the branches. By half past four the job was done, and only the twigs and chips remained to be collected into a box for kindling wood.

'I've got two blisters,' laughed Emily, holding out her hands.

'I haven't,' said Billy proudly, surveying his own grimy hands.

'We deserve some tea,' said his old headmistress, leading the way to the house.

It was over home-made fruit cake and steaming cups of tea that Billy told his tale. He had never felt any shyness in Emily's presence, and their shared labours that afternoon made it easier for him to speak, as Emily had intended.

There was little need for her to probe. The boy was glad to find someone to talk to, and the new problems came tumbling out. They were not new, of course, to Emily Davis. She had seen many children in the same predicament. There were very few, in fact, who went on to the large Caxley schools from Springbourne, who did not find the journey, the pace of work and the numbers surrounding them, as daunting as young Billy did.

And then came the sorry tale of the conkers. If Billy had expected sympathy, he was to be surprised. Emily took the account of his discomfiture with brisk matter-of-factness. 'If "no conkers" is a school rule – although I doubt it – you must just abide by it. Nothing to stop you enjoying a game at home, anyway. And as for that prefect, well, you'll find people like that everywhere, and he was only trying to do his duty, poor young man.'

'Poor young man', indeed, thought Billy resentfully! But he had the sense to remain silent.

Emily refilled his tea-cup and went on to talk, as though at random, of the difficulties of adjusting oneself to new situations. Billy was soon aware that he was not the only person to have suffered growing pains. It was true, as Miss Davis said, that one's world grew bigger every so often. It was an ordeal to leave home for one's first school; it was a bigger one to change to a larger school, as he had just done.

'And then you'll plunge into a deeper pool still, if you go to a university,' said Emily, 'and probably nearly drown when you dive into the world of work after that! But you'll survive, Billy, you'll see, and be able to help a great many other young people who are busy jumping from one pool to the next and floundering now and again!'

It was all said so light-heartedly that it was not until many years later that Billy realised how skilfully the lesson had been imparted. At the time, he was only conscious of comfort and the resurgence of his natural high spirits, and put both down to energetic sawing in the open air, and Emily's excellent fruit cake.

At the gate, Billy turned and surveyed the old familiar playground next door.

'I wish I were back,' he said impulsively.

Emily shook her head, smiling.

'You don't really. You're much too big a fish for that little pond now, and I think you are beginning to know it.'

She looked at Billy thoughtfully.

'What was the name of that prefect?'

Billy told her. She was silent for a minute, and then seemed to come to a decision.

'I'm going to tell you something which you must keep to yourself, but I think you can do it, and I think it will help you.'

'I can keep a secret,' promised Billy.

'That boy went from Fairacre School to Caxley. The family moved later, but this is what I want you to know. Miss Clare told me that he was so upset in his first term that his parents thought he might have to leave. From what you tell me, he seems to be keeping afloat in his bigger pond now.'

'He's unsinkable!' commented Billy ruefully.

'Well, think about it. I've only told you because I believe it might help you to understand people. But not a word to anyone, Billy.'

'Not a word,' he echoed solemnly, and ran home with half a crown as wages in his hand, and new-found hope in his heart.

Wisps of white mist were drifting in from the sea as Billy Dove drove his Land-Rover over the rutted site to his office.

The sun was almost blotted out now, faintly discernible now and again, riding moon-like through the ragged clouds. Billy hated this sea-mist, which local people called 'the haar', which swept in unpredictably and wrapped the countryside in icy veils.

He shivered as he entered the small granite house where his office was situated on the ground floor. He was the first to arrive. His colleagues would be coming within the next quarter of an hour, but now he had the little house to himself, and had time to think.

He took out the letter and read it again. Taormina! And Mary! Gazing into the swirling whiteness outside, he longed to return to the sunshine, the flowers, the cypress trees – and, above all, to the warmth and love of Mary. It would be so easy to return, and have a week or two of utter happiness in the sun. The work here could go on under young Bannister's eye without much effort. God, it was tempting!

He stood up suddenly, hands in pockets, and went to the window. Coins jingled as he turned his loose change over and over in his nervousness.

This was a situation he must face alone. No wise old Miss Davis to turn to now.

He gave an impatient snort of derision. What would Emily Davis know, anyway, of a man's feelings? Much use she would be to him with a problem like this. Her advice would come out ready-made, as automatically as a packet from a slot machine.

'Your duty, my boy, is to your wife and children! The rest is temptation. It is SIN, put before you by the devil himself.'

How simple life must have been to those old Victorians with their rigid rules of conduct! But how much they must have missed!

He faced about, turning his back upon the blank whiteness now shrouding the hill side in impenetrable clammy fog.

Nevertheless, it was the only course to take. He had made up his mind to stay in Scotland as soon as he read the letter. Temptation, the devil, Emily Davis and all the other faintly ridiculous issues which clouded his mind, at the moment, as confusingly as the mist outside, made no difference to his decision. He had made the break with Mary. He would not go back.

He had a sudden memory of Sarah that morning, laughing in her blue and white cotton frock, and of John's conspiratorial wink across the playground.

He smiled as he drew a piece of writing paper towards him. Young Bannister would see Sicily for the first time. He would remain in Scotland.

He banged on the stamp as his assistant's car drew up outside, and went outside to meet him. It was like stepping naked into a wet mackintosh. God, what a climate!

Some men, thought Billy Dove, would say he was out of his mind to turn down the opportunity of leaving it. Perhaps he was. Who knows?

Ah well, the decision was made and, bitter though it was, it was the right one. He began to smile.

'What's the joke?' said his assistant.

'I'm trying to decide if I've come to my senses – or lost them completely,' said Billy.

The assistant raised his eyebrows, and Billy laughed ruefully.

'One thing, Miss Davis would approve.'

He clapped his bewildered colleague on the shoulder.

'Come along, son. We've work to do.'

13 Mrs Pringle Disapproves

THE village of Fairacre is some two miles from Beech Green, but news – particularly bad news – travels swiftly in the country, and Emily's death was heard of within a few hours of its happening.

The people of Fairacre knew Emily well, but their first concern was for Dolly Clare who had taught them, and their children, for so many years at Fairacre School.

As children, Emily and Dolly had attended Fairacre School, and later had taught there as pupil teachers. Dolly had remained there for the rest of her teaching life, whilst Emily had gone first to Caxley and then to Springbourne. When Springbourne School closed, as a result of the 1944 act, Emily was transferred to a Caxley school, and lived with a younger brother for whom she kept house. She was glad when he married, and she was free to join Dolly Clare. In the last happy years of their shared retirement, the two old ladies had frequently visited Fairacre, and indeed they were as well known there, by young and old, as in Beech Green.

'I'd have taken a bet on Dolly Clare going first,' observed Mr Willet to Mrs Pringle. Mr Willet is a man of many parts. He is school caretaker, sexton, verger, local nurseryman and a pillar of strength to all needing practical advice on such matters as faulty plumbing, pruning roses, tiling a roof and coping generally with a householder's problems.

Mrs Pringle is as gloomy as Mr Willet is sunny. She acts as school cleaner, is the bane of her headmistress's life, and a terror and scourge to all those with dirt on their shoes. Mrs Pringle is one of this world's martyrs, but one who certainly does not suffer in silence.

On this mellow afternoon of autumn sunshine, Mrs Pringle encountered Mr Willet as she made her way homeward from washing up the school dinner plates and cutlery.

St Patrick's clock had struck two, and Mr Willet was perched on a ladder picking early black plums from a tree in his front garden. He was suitably impressed with the gravity of Mrs Pringle's news of Emily Davis's going, and dismounted the ladder to converse over the gate.

Mr Willet knew what was fitting. One could not carry on a conversation on such a serious matter when engaged on plum-picking, ten feet above ground. It would be disrespectful to the dead, and an affront to Mrs Pringle.

'Yes, I'd have taken a bet on Dolly Clare going first,' he repeated, pushing back his cap. 'She'll miss her, you know. Anyone with her?'

Flattered by his attention, Mrs Pringle launched into her narrative. It was not often that Mr Willet treated her words with such respect. She made the most of this rare occasion, and propped her black oil cloth bag against the gate, at her feet, as if she intended to be some time imparting her news.

Mr Willet, anxious though he was to hear it, watched the gesture with some foreboding. He had some hoeing to do, after the plum-picking, and some seeds to water. Mrs Pringle, launched upon the tide of her story, could take an unconscionable time getting to its end, as he knew well.

'I thought, the last time I saw Miss Davis,' began Mrs

Pringle lugubriously, 'as she was on the wane. Funny how you gets to know. There's a look about folks, as no doubt you've noticed, Mr Willet.'

'Can't say I have,' replied Mr Willet shortly, his eyes roving to the plum tree.

'Ah well!' conceded Mrs Pringle, with a certain ghoulish smugness, 'there's some of us more in tune with the Other World. You gets to recognise the Hand of Death, before it's even fallen. Miss Davis had that look – just as though she was seeing the Farther Shore.'

'Stummer-cake, more like,' said Mr Willet sturdily. He did not hold with morbid fancies, and in these realms of psychic fantasy Mrs Pringle could lose herself for a good ten minutes, if not checked. Dear knows when he'd get the seeds watered, at this rate!

Mrs Pringle ignored his coarse interjection. It was not often that she had such a valuable captive audience. She returned to her theme with all the concentration of a terrier with a rat.

'I saw the same look on my poor mother's face the night before she died. "She won't last another day," I told my husband. "She got that hollow-cheeked look".'

'You should have put her teeth in again,' observed Mr Willet.

'And next morning I found her cold,' continued Mrs Pringle undaunted. 'She looked a young woman. At Peace. We had them words put on her stone actually.'

'I might get my bike out later on and see if I can do anything for Dolly Clare,' said Mr Willet.

'With Emily Davis still in the house?' cried Mrs Pringle, scandalised. 'Where's your sense of fitness?'

'Dolly Clare might be glad of a hand. You can do with an old friend when you've taken a knock like that.'

'They say the Annetts are keeping an eye on her,' said Mrs Pringle. 'Very good thing too. She's none too strong, is Dolly Clare. A shock like this could be the death of her.'

There was a glint of pleasurable anticipation in the old terror's eye which riled Mr Willet.

'Don't start thinking of double funerals,' he said tartly. Mrs Pringle bridled. Her thoughts had indeed strayed into this delectable and dramatic field. She changed her tactics swiftly before Mr Willet escaped from her clutches and returned to his plum-picking.

'The very idea!' she protested, her double chin wobbling indignantly. 'As a matter of fact, I was recalling how good Miss Davis was to my brother-in-law – the one at Springbourne. She often found him a little job when times were hard. You knows what a family he had.'

Mr Willet began to despair of ever getting his jobs done. He was about to make a firm break, and risk Mrs Pringle's displeasure, when he saw help at hand.

A large shabby pram, squeaking to high heaven, approached from the Springbourne direction. A slatternly girl, with dishevelled red hair, pushed it, a toddler clinging to her skirts.

Mr Willet's spirits rose.

'Here's one of the family now,' he said joyfully. 'I'll get back to work.'

With remarkable speed for one so thickset, he remounted the step ladder.

It was Minnie Pringle who approached. She was still known to the neighbourhood as Minnie Pringle, although she was now a married woman. A feckless body, 'not quite all there', as people said, she had produced three children before marriage, and two since. Her husband was much older than she was, a dour widower with a number of young children of his own. The combined families occupied a dilapidated semi-detached villa on the outskirts of Springbourne and seemed to thrive under Minnie's erratic care.

The house reeked permanently of neck-of-mutton stew, which was the only dish which Minnie had mastered over the years. This, with plenty of potatoes, innumerable sliced white loaves from a Caxley supermarket, and pots of strong sweet tea, constituted the household's diet. They all seemed to thrive on it.

Their clothes were given to them by kindly neighbours or bought for a few shillings at local jumble sales. Minnie's husband reckoned that his wages as a road-sweeper paid the rent of their shabby house, provided the food and left him ten shillings a week for beer and cigarettes.

Minnie found the arrangement perfectly satisfactory. After her haphazard upbringing it all seemed a model of household efficiency.

She greeted her aunt boisterously, sniffing the while.

'We've bin in your place, but you wasn't there.'

'Not surprising, is it?' said Mrs Pringle.

Sarcasm was lost upon Minnie.

'Just going to the Post Office to get me family.'

Mrs Pringle rightly translated this as 'family allowances', and snorted. This was a sore point.

'It's people like you, Minnie, as keeps people like me *poor*! About time you stopped having babies and expecting us hard-working folk to keep 'em for you.'

'I don't ask 'em to come,' replied Minnie, tossing her unkempt head.

'You don't do much to stop 'em as far as I can see,' boomed her aunt. She looked with disfavour upon the toddler who was wiping his nose on his coat cuff.

'I'll drop in on my way back,' said Minnie cheerfully. She was not one to harbour grudges. Mrs Pringle sighed heavily, picked up her black oil cloth bag, and faced the inevitable.

'I'll go and put the kettle on,' she said resignedly. 'Don't dilly-dally now, Minnie. I've plenty to do when I get home, so don't keep me hanging about.'

Mr Willet, high among the branches, echoed this sentiment, and watched Mrs Pringle's squat figure stumping homeward into the distance.

* * *

What a family! What a disgrace to decent people! thought Mrs Pringle, setting out the cups and saucers on a tin tray. Of course, they were only relations by marriage, but even so!

Mrs Pringle shuddered at the thought of her husband's younger brother Josh. Nothing but a byword, as far as Caxley, and further. The police of three counties had been after him, for one thing or other. If it wasn't petty thieving in the market, it was breaking and entering, or being picked up dead drunk. Or else it was poaching, thought Mrs Pringle, putting out a few broken biscuits for the children.

Yes, poaching. And Miss Davis knew a bit about that too, come to think of it. It wasn't the sort of story you would tell to Mr Willet, say, but it just showed you that Emily Davis had her head screwed on, and her heart in the right place too.

The sight of that dratted girl Minnie had brought back the memory very sharply. Mrs Pringle shifted the kettle to the side of the stove, picked up her crochet work, and sat down, with a sigh, to await her niece's coming with what patience she could muster.

It had all happened when Minnie was eight or nine years of age – the scruffiest and most scatter-brained pupil in Emily Davis's class at Springbourne.

The child's work was atrociously done. Her writing always appeared to have been executed with a crossed nib dipped heavily in black honey. The pages bore the imprint of dirty fingers, despite Emily's insistence on frequent washings in the lobby.

After super-human efforts by Emily, Minnie had begun to read. Figure work seemed to be completely beyond her. Numbers to five had some reality for the child, and Emily had hopes of her comprehending those up to ten in the future. A realist, Emily faced the fact that double figures would probably always be beyond Minnie's ken. In this she was to be proved right.

Emily concentrated on Minnie's newly-acquired reading ability, substituted a pencil for the pen with the permanently crossed nib, and began to see the child making some headway.

It was not surprising that she was so backward. Her father, Josh Pringle, was the black sheep of his family, constantly in trouble, easily led by his dubious companions, and a mighty consumer of beer whenever he could afford to buy it. Occasionally he obtained work as a labourer, but his income was mainly derived from petty thieving, or from keeping a watch for the police whilst his cronies were 'doing a job'.

Minnie's mother was a brow-beaten wisp of a woman, prematurely grey, who looked twice her age, and had long since given up the struggle to keep her home and children tidy.

Meals were erratic. Sometimes she cooked a rabbit stew for the family, or a simple pie or pudding. More often, the children were told to help themselves to bread and jam from the cupboard. There was no money to buy meat, but Josh's poaching supplied them with a certain amount of nourishment in the form of snared rabbits and hares. Now and again, he took his old gun and picked off a roosting pheasant on Sir Edmund Hurley's estate. Bob Dixon, the gamekeeper, was Josh's implacable enemy.

One night, in October, Bob Dixon sat in 'The Crown' at Springbourne. He had a pint of draught bitter on the table in the corner, and his companion was the local policeman, Danny Goss, off duty.

Bob was a taciturn individual, and made few friends. He was

not particularly fond of Danny Goss, but at least they had a common enemy – poachers. And another thing, Danny Goss played a hard game of dominoes, and this Bob relished. They were in the middle of a game when old Tim Ryan came in and sidled up to them.

'Evening, Dan. Evening, Bob.'

They acknowledged his greetings with grunts, resenting interruption of the game.

Tim watched a few moves in silence, and then spoke in a low tone.

'There's some shootin' going on up Narrow Copse. Thought you should know.'

Bob stood up immediately. Danny finished his drink, put back the dominoes into their greasy box, and followed suit. Bob put a florin on the counter and nodded towards Tim.

'Give the old boy a drink,' he said to the barman.

The two men emerged into the cold night air. It was a light night, for it was full moon. Clouds covered its face, but a silvery diffused brightness made visibility easy. A shot rang out as they emerged, and without speaking they ran, one behind the other, along the grass verge which muffled the sound of their footsteps.

The small copse sloped at an angle to the road, and met it about a quarter of a mile from the pub. The two men entered the wood, and stood motionless for a minute or two.

They heard the cracking of twigs nearby and held their breath. From behind the oak tree which screened them they had a view of a small clearing. Across this, gun in hand, went the figure of a man, followed by another.

'Now,' whispered Bob.

He and the policeman ran into the clearing.

'Beat it, Arth!' shouted one of the men. They ran in opposite directions, crashing through the undergrowth, pursued by the game-keeper and policeman.

Bob Dixon caught his man within fifty yards of the clearing. But as he made a grab for his jacket, the man turned and smote Bob with such viciousness in the face that the game-keeper fell to the ground with a cry of pain.

The man ran off, as Bob was struggling to his feet. At the same time Danny Goss returned.

'He had a bike in the hedge,' he said bitterly. 'But I'd take a bet it was Arthur Coggs from Fairacre. Your chap called out "Arth", didn't he?'

Bob, staunching his bloodied nose, nodded.

'And I'm pretty sure mine was Josh Pringle. I'm going over there now.'

'I'll come with you,' said Danny grimly. 'They're a right pair, those two.'

Josh Pringle sped for home by a roundabout route, two fat cock pheasants thumping his thighs as he ran. He was in roaring high spirits. He had outwitted his enemy and he had paid off old scores with that satisfying crash on his nose.

Full of triumph, Josh did not fully realise the danger which he was in. The thought that Bob Dixon or Danny Goss might pursue him further that night did not seriously worry him. Tomorrow morning, perhaps, there might be a few awkward questions to face if they found him, but surely they'd had enough for tonight?

He was a little perplexed, though, as he ran, about the hasty disposal of the birds. He wasn't going to hide them in the woods or hedges. He'd been fleeced that way before by unscrupulous neighbours. Besides, Bob knew every hiding place as well as he did. Better by far to get them home and cooked as soon as possible. The gentry might prefer their game hung. Poachers could not afford the time.

'Get 'em under the crust,' he had told his wife often enough. 'No one can tell what's under the crust.' There would be pheasant pie tomorrow – enough for all.

He found his wife kneeling before the fire, poker in hand, when he burst in breathlessly.

'Don't rake that out, gal,' he told her roughly, tugging the birds from his poacher's pockets. 'We got to get these plucked straight away. Had a job gettin' away from Bob Dixon.'

'You ain't been seen, 'ave you, Josh?' quavered his wife, Agnes.

'He didn't 'ave no time to see anythink,' responded Josh, beginning to strip feathers expertly. He threw the second bird on to his wife's lap. 'Him and that great lump Goss come after us, but we give 'em the slip. You keep your mouth shut if they turns up tomorrow. Don't know nothin', see?'

Agnes nodded dumbly, her hands busy with the feathers. She took a sheet of newspaper from the table and spread it at her feet to catch the bronze plumage as it fell. Josh's bird lolled upon the table top, its long tail feathers brushing his jacket.

The fire whispered as they worked in silence. Josh raised his head suddenly.

'By gum, there's someone outside,' he whispered, gazing at the dirty drawn curtains. 'Nip upstairs with these while I burn the feathers. If it's Bob Dixon – '

His face was dark with fury. He thrust the two half-plucked birds into his wife's arms, and began to roll up the newspapers.

'Get on upstairs,' he told her in a fierce whisper.

'But where can I put 'em?' squeaked poor Agnes.

'Bung 'em under the bed clothes with the kids, you great fool,' hissed Josh, stuffing the bundles of paper and feathers to the back of the fire.

Agnes crept away, up the box staircase to the room above, on her errand. A strong smell of burning feathers floated about the room, and Josh cursed as he picked up a stray feather or two and added it to the blaze.

A thunderous knocking came at the door. Josh ignored it. By now the bundles on the fire were black and almost burnt through. He blew on the fire to hasten its work.

The knocking came again, and then a voice.

'Open up, Josh Pringle. Police here.'

Josh swore violently, and stirred the bundles until they disintegrated. He put on some chips of wood from a wooden box nearby, and watched them burst into flame.

He approached the door and opened it.

The sight of Bob Dixon's swollen and bloodied nose frightened him. One eye too was blackening fast. He had not realised that he had done so much damage. Too late now to worry about that, he told himself, putting on an innocent expression.

'What's all this about?' he asked truculently. 'Kicking up a fuss like this! We've got kids asleep, I'll have you know. And one's got spots – scarlet fever or summat, we reckon. Only just got off to sleep, he has.'

'We'd like to come in,' said Goss.

'I daresay,' responded Josh, with spirit. 'But I don't want you.' The longer he could keep them from the reek of burning feathers, the better.

'There's such a thing as obstructing an officer of the law in the execution of his duty,' said Goss ponderously. 'I want a word with you on one or two matters.'

'Such as?'

'Such as poaching,' broke in Bob Dixon warmly. 'And knocking me down, you ruddy swine.'

'Leave this to me,' said Goss, to his hot-headed friend. 'I've reason to believe,' he said to Josh, with a return to his official manner, 'that you have articles in this house which are not your property. I'd like to take a look round.'

'Got a search warrant?' queried Josh. 'I knows me rights.'

'There'll be one tomorrow morning,' promised Goss. There was a menacing ring in his tone. 'If you've got nothing to hide, what are you hedging for?'

Josh appeared to waver. By now the feathers should have vanished. The smell too was practically non-existent. He opened the door grudgingly.

'Come on in then, if you must. You won't find nothin' here, I'm warning you.'

Danny Goss made straight for the fire and stirred it with the poker. He saw at once that he was too late. But on the shabby mat he noticed two small brown feathers.

'Pheasant's, eh?' he said. Josh began to bluster.

'Don't make me laugh. Folks like us don't 'ave pheasants. We leaves that to chaps like Bob Dixon 'ere.'

At this point Agnes opened the door from the staircase and entered timidly.

'These 'ere feathers,' said Josh loudly, giving his witless Agnes time to sum up the situation. 'They're from that old hen your mum gave us. That's right, ain't it?'

'Yes,' whispered Agnes. Growing bolder, she added: ' 'Twas

a Rhode Island Red. Finished laying. My mum give it to me to boil for the kids' dinner.'

'That's right,' agreed Josh, nodding approval. 'I told you, they've bin poorly. One's all over spots, ain't he, Ag?'

'Spots?' cried Agnes, her hand flying to her mouth. 'Who's got – ?'

Josh broke in loudly. Lord, was she thick? He'd have to get it through to her somehow, or they'd be upstairs in two shakes.

'Our Tommy. Just bin up to see him, you should know. I was telling these chaps we wondered if it was scarlet fever. Don't want them catching nothin'.'

'That's right,' said Agnes wonderingly.

'You have a look down here,' said Josh, throwing open his arms expansively. 'Look in the washus, out the back, in the privy – we ain't got nothing to hide here.'

'Take a look, if you've a mind,' said Goss to Dixon. The gamekeeper went through the kitchen to the ramshackle outbuildings at the rear of the house. They could hear him opening doors and stumbling among the heap of logs in the corner of the wash-house.

Danny Goss raked the living room with an experienced eye. There were few places to hide a pheasant here. He'd lay a wager they were upstairs, but without a search warrant he was helpless. Nevertheless, he tried.

'I'd like a look upstairs. I won't disturb the children.'

'You can wait then! Them kids is asleep, I tell you. Can't you take a chap's word?'

'No,' said Goss briefly.

'I lets you in,' protested Josh, with a fine show of affronted innocence, 'and shows you downstairs. I'll show you more!'

With a magnificent gesture, he wrenched open the door to

the box staircase, displaying bare wooden stairs, much splintered, and the vanishing tail of a startled mouse.

'There! See anythink? Any pheasants, partridges, hares, or whatever old codswallop you reckons I've got here?'

'It's upstairs, Josh,' said Danny calmly.

'Don't talk so daft! When could I 'ave got it? I bin sittin' 'ere all evening. That's the truth. Eh, Ag?'

Agnes nodded obediently. She was wondering how soon it would be before the children awoke and discovered their gruesome bed-fellows, and how loudly they would scream the news.

As if sensing her thoughts, Josh prudently closed the door. Bob Dixon returned, his discoloured face wearing a sullen look.

'Dam' all,' he said briefly.

Danny Goss, knowing he was beaten, prepared to leave, but not without a stern warning.

'Bob saw his assailant, you know,' he said. 'He'll give evidence in court.'

'Who else saw?' asked Josh pertinently.

'You should know,' said Bob hotly.

'I bin sittin' here all evening,' repeated Josh with emphasis.

'You'll have to prove that.'

'Me brother come up with the paper about nine,' said Josh glibly. His brother would agree to anything Josh suggested. He was smaller than Josh. 'And Ag will vouch for me.'

'You'll need to do better than that,' observed Danny Goss, opening the door. 'We'll be back.'

Josh accompanied them to the rickety gate, and watched them until they were out of sight. He returned to hear the frenzied wailing of a child.

'Mum! Mum! There's chickens in our bed! Dead 'uns,

mum, but they're pricking us something awful! Mum! Mum!'

Agnes started to climb aloft.

'Chuck 'em under our bed till morning,' advised her husband. 'We'll finish 'em off before his lordship comes back. All this bloomin' fuss,' he growled. 'It's enough to make a chap go straight.'

It so happened that no charge was made by the police against Josh on this occasion. Evidence was flimsy. No firm case could really be made. It would be Bob Dixon's word against Josh's. But both the gamekeeper and the policeman vowed to keep a sharp eye on Josh Pringle, and to make sure that next time he transgressed then justice would be done.

Rumours flew about, of course, but Josh played the injured innocent and weathered this particular storm with some skill. In the privacy of his own home he boasted of his triumph, but he kept a still tongue abroad, and congratulated himself on having deceived his neighbours. He would not have been so smug if he had known that Emily Davis knew all.

Some days after the poaching incident, Emily set her class an essay to write. She knew, from bitter experience, that it was little use to expect flights of fancy from the majority of the children. They were, on the whole, unimaginative and ploddingly prosaic. As she wanted, on this occasion, as lengthy a piece of writing as they could manage, she gave them a simple, down-to-earth subject which all could tackle.

My Favourite Meal

she wrote in a fair copper-plate hand on the blackboard. There were murmurs of approval from the victims.

'And I want two or three pages,' said Emily briskly. 'Don't

worry too much about spelling and writing this afternoon. Just show me how much you can do.'

After a few preliminary enquiries, such as: 'Must we draw a line under the heading?' and 'Is jam tarts all one word?' which Emily dismissed smartly, the class settled down to literary composition with all its accompanying sighs and groans.

The children worked well, and at playtime Emily collected their books. They were left in a pile on her desk, and were carried across to the school house for marking that evening.

Halfway through the pile she came across Minnie Pringle's effort.

'Well done, Minnie,' murmured Emily, surveying the laboriously pencilled page. 'The longest essay to date. If only I can read it – '

The spelling and the writing rendered Minnie's composition well-nigh incomprehensible. Minnie had no use for punctuation, so that the whole narrative appeared as one long breathless sentence.

Translated, it read as follows:

My Favourite Meal

Best of all I likes pheasant pie what mum makes with pastry to hide whats inside as my dad tells her with gravy my dad finds them up the woods they just walks about the other night some men come and my mum put them pheasants in us kids bed to keep them warm she said they tickled us and had fleas we had two pies one Wednesday one Thursday today it was bread and sauce pheasant pie is best

Emily who had heard the rumours smiled at this artless account. But it was Minnie's best effort to date. She was very pleased with the child. Taking out her box of gold stars, Emily stuck one securely at the end of the essay. 'For good work,' she wrote beside it.

Gold stars were rarely given. They were much prized by those who earned them. Emily usually allowed the child to take home the work to show the proud parents. In this case, Emily thought, it would be wiser not to do so. She could imagine Josh's reaction to his daughter's innocent admission.

Minnie was scarlet to the roots of her red hair when she found her star.

'Can I take it home, miss? Can I?' she begged.

Emily spoke gently.

'I've put a star on a piece of paper, Minnie. You can take that home to show them. Tell them it was for a good piece of writing.'

She wondered if she should warn the child not to mention the subject matter of the essay. It would seem rather hard to Minnie if Josh's leather belt greeted her success.

'Just for good work,' repeated Emily carefully. Minnie nodded, dumb with delight.

Emily need not have worried. The gold star was given a cursory glance by Agnes and no attention at all by Josh. Not that this worried Minnie. She expected nothing more at home. Her hour of triumph had been at school. But she would have liked to take her book home, nevertheless.

It had been Minnie's aunt, Mrs Pringle herself, Fairacre School's formidable cleaner, who had warned Minnie about disclosing the theme of the essay.

The child had shown her the famous star soon after it had been won.

'What was it for?' asked Mrs Pringle, and listened, aghast,

as she was told. She had already heard the rumours about that fateful night, and suspected that they were true. This confirmed them.

'Have you told anyone else?' she asked.

'No, auntie.'

'Then don't. Your dad'll leather you if he finds out.'

'Miss Davis knows.'

'Maybe. But Miss Davis won't tell.'

The child had seemed bewildered. Mrs Pringle often wondered if she realised the reason for keeping quiet. She doubted it. Minnie was as dim as a dark night, thought her aunt, but at least she'd kept her mouth shut after that, and Josh had got away with it.

But not for long, remembered Mrs Pringle, with satisfaction. A month or two later he had been caught with a carrier-bag stuffed with stolen silver. With a string of other cases taken into consideration, this escapade earned him six months in jail. Agnes and the children missed the rabbits, but the house was wonderfully peaceful.

> 'Though mills of God grind slowly
> Yet they grind exceeding small,'

Mrs Pringle hummed to herself, recollecting Josh's imprisonment with pleasure.

The squeaking of Minnie's pram became apparent, and Mrs Pringle warmed the teapot. She must let Minnie know about poor Miss Davis. It ought to upset her nicely.

That is, if she remembered her at all, she thought, with some asperity. Knowing Minnie she wouldn't be surprised to find Miss Davis had been forgotten completely.

Sighing deeply, she reached for the tea-caddy.

14 Peeping Tom

MR WILLET filled his basket, stepped carefully down the ladder and went into the kitchen. His wife was ironing, a clothes horse beside her laden with Mr Willet's striped pyjamas and substantial underwear, and some snowy sheets and pillow cases. The comfortable smell of warm linen filled the air.

'Old Misery Pringle's just stopped by,' said Mr Willet disrespectfully. 'Got bad news as usual, and enjoying it.'

'What's that?'

'Emily Davis has gone.'

'No! Why, she was at church the Sunday before last!'

'She'll be going again, poor soul,' said Mr Willet. 'And for the last time.'

He watched his wife sprinkling some water over the handkerchiefs.

'Thought I might pop up and see if Dolly Clare wants anything.'

'Oh, I wouldn't do that just yet!' protested Mrs Willet. 'Leave it a day or two.'

Women! thought Mr Willet. All the same, maybe she was right.

He puffed out his stained moustache with a resigned sigh.

'Maybe that's best,' he agreed, and went off to his hoeing.

* * *

Emily's death had stirred memories for Mrs Pringle of her reprehensible brother-in-law. The event had stirred memories too for Bob Willet, memories which even now filled him with some shame. Both Mrs Pringle and Mr Willet kept their recollections to themselves with much prudence, but this did not render them any less painful.

It had all started when Bob Willet was at the impressionable age of seven. He lived then, with his four brothers and sisters, in a little house between Springbourne and Fairacre, and attended Fairacre School.

At that time the schoolmaster was a dreamy idealistic fellow called Hope. He was looked upon as 'a bit of a milk-sop' by the parents, but the children liked him. For one thing, he believed in reading them stories, which children always enjoy. Those who are attentive learn a great deal. Those who close their ears and daydream can get away with such behaviour with impunity. One way or another, storytime is universally popular.

Young Bob Willet was one of those who did attend. Mr Hope read them all manner of tales from the myths of Greece to passages from *Midshipman Easy*. He also read some of Andrew Lang's fairy tales, and it was these which impressed Bob particularly. He became fascinated by witches.

It so happened that a poor old crone called Lucy Kelly, then about eighty years of age, lived alone in a tumbledown cottage near the Willets' home. She was a fearsome sight, with one long eye-tooth overhanging her bottom lip, and tangled grey locks escaping from the man's black trilby hat which she usually wore.

Her clothes were deplorable, her cottage worse. Neighbours had long since given up trying to help her, for she was half-mad, muttering to herself constantly, and violent if provoked. Bob Willet had heard her called 'an old witch' by several people in the village. No doubt it was said in jest, but the boy believed it.

How could he prove it? Fearfully, he put his problem to Ted Pickett, a boy a little older than himself. Mrs Willet did not approve of the Picketts. She considered them dirty and untruthful, and wished her Bob had made friends elsewhere. But nothing could be done without giving offence, and Ted Pickett called for Bob, on his way to Fairacre School from Springbourne, and Mrs Willet could only hope that time would part them one day.

Ted Pickett was something of a hero to Bob. He was an intrepid tree climber and good at football. What more do you ask of a hero when you are a seven-year-old boy?

Bob half-hoped that Ted would give him some comfort when he told him about Lucy. It would have been a relief to have been laughed to scorn for harbouring such a wrong notion. But Ted Pickett did not laugh and Bob did not know whether to feel glad or not. According to Ted Pickett, Lucy might well be a witch. The only way to prove it was to catch her flying on a broomstick at the full moon. On that Ted Pickett was positive.

'Come with me?' asked Bob.

'No fear!' said his hero. 'I'm scared of anything like that!'

It was not very reassuring, but Bob's curiosity got the better of his fear, and one night of full moon he crept from the house and made his way to Lucy Kelly's cottage.

Everything seemed eerie in the silvery light. It was warm and still. The harvest had been gathered, and stooks of wheat stood in the stubbly fields, throwing sharp pointed shadows. The scents of the fruitful sun-warmed earth hung everywhere.

Bob approached Lucy's house stealthily, his heart in his mouth. The front of the shabby place was in full moonlight, and to Bob's horror he saw a stout besom broom lodged against the wooden lean-to at one end of the cottage.

So she had got a broomstick! For two pins, Bob would have run home, but having come so far he braced himself to investigate further.

The garden was full of waist-high docks and nettles, but by keeping close to the house he managed to make progress. Fearfully, he peeped into one grimy window. By the light of the moon he could see some ramshackle furniture. All was silent. Where was Lucy? Was she already preparing herself for a midnight flight?

He gazed spell-bound into the room, noting the battered kettle on the hob, the broken armchair with the stuffing oozing from its sagging seat, and the opened tin of condensed milk standing on the table with a spoon lodged in it.

There was something wholly fascinating in seeing a private life so plainly disclosed. Young Bob had never visited a theatre or he might have recognised the excitement which mounted in him, despite his fear. Here was a stage and although no actors could be seen upon it, a drama must take place.

Action was about to begin. The clock of distant St Patrick's began to strike twelve, each note floating clearly across the tranquil countryside. The boy grew cold with mingled terror and excitement. It was midnight – the time for witches' flights.

At that moment, a dark shape rolled from some low couch hard against the wall where Bob stood. It had been hidden from his sight as it was immediately below the window through which he was looking.

It was Lucy! Dry-mouthed, Bob watched her throw a black shawl round her shoulders and make for the door. It was enough for the terrified boy.

Lucy was off to her broomstick!

Bob Willet fled.

You may think that such an experience would scotch a boy's desire for private investigation, but funnily enough, it seemed to whet young Bob Willet's appetite for more. That glimpse into someone else's life affected the boy deeply. He always loved a story, and was to become a fine raconteur in later life, but this was something better than a story. It was experience at first hand – real people occupying a real place, an actual story unfolding while he watched.

He took to loitering past lighted cottage windows, and treasuring the glimpses of life within. Here was a baby being bathed by the fire. Here was a man setting down a foaming jug of beer on the dresser. Here was an old woman, nodding by the fire, her head on one side and mouth open, while the cat lapped milk from a jug on the table. These little vignettes fascinated the child.

He did not speak about them for some time, knowing full well that his mother would scold him for prying. But one day, he mentioned his new game to Ted Pickett.

By now it was winter-time and lamps were lit at tea-time. Children were told to be sure to be in by dark. Mrs Willet was a stickler for obedience, and one Saturday afternoon young Bob was allowed to go and play at Ted Pickett's only on the strict understanding that he was home before dusk.

The two boys spent a blissful afternoon kicking an old ball about a muddy field. Dusk began to fall and the cottage windows gleamed golden as the lamps were lit. Bob Willet, seeing them, reminded Ted Pickett of his game.

'Bet you wouldn't dare to look in Miss Davis's window,' challenged Ted. The village school stood nearby, and the school house adjoined it, surrounded on three sides by grass which Emily kept shorn with a hand mower which frequently went wrong.

Bob's heart gave a jump. Emily Davis was someone to be respected, even feared. Supposing she saw him at the window?

On the other hand, Ted had dared him. And Ted was older and bigger. If he did not take up the challenge, Ted might put an end to the friendship. There were plenty of boys at school who would be proud to take his place at Ted Pickett's side. Swiftly, the younger boy made up his mind.

'Who said I wouldn't dare?' he boasted, his heart fluttering. 'Come on then. Let's go over now.'

In the grey moth-light between day and night, the two went stealthily across the road from the field. A light burned in the little sitting room of the school house. They could see the lamp quite clearly, standing centrally on the table, for the window was a low one.

'Get round the side,' whispered Ted, 'and creep along below the window level.'

Bob led the way, Ted following. They skirted a row of lilac bushes which grew between the school playground and Emily's garden. It grew darker every minute. The two crouched down in an angle formed by two walls, waiting for an opportune moment.

A farm labourer, with his dog, clumped along the lane, only

a few yards from them. The dog raised its muzzle, sniffing the air, and for one awful moment Bob thought that they would be discovered. But the man was intent on getting home, and calling his dog to heel, he made off down the road.

Two small children then appeared, and took a long time to pass the school premises. Then one of their neighbours, who had been wooding, trundled an old pram piled high with dead branches, along the lane. Bob was terrified that she might see him. His mother would soon hear about it, if she did.

The thought of his mother made him more nervous still. It was time he was home. It was cold squatting there, and getting dangerously late. Now he had taken up Ted's challenge he must get on with it – and the sooner it was over, the better.

Now the lane was clear, and Bob nudged Ted.

'Coming?' he whispered.

Ted nodded.

Bent low, young Bob crept along the front of the school house until he was squarely below the lighted window. Ted joined him, and they sat on their haunches side by side.

Bob listened. Not a sound disturbed the twilight. Face to the wall, he raised himself, inch by inch, until his eyes were level with the lowest pane of glass. Beside him, Ted Pickett followed suit.

There was only one person in the room, and that was Emily's mother. They could see the top of her white head above the back of the armchair. An open book lay on a stool beside the chair, and a large ball of white wool. They could see the old lady's right hand moving dextrously and rhythmically as she worked at her crochet. At that very moment, just as the usual magic was beginning to work for Bob, a terrible blow smote him, and he banged heads with Ted Pickett violently. Both boys tumbled to the ground.

Through the stars born of this sudden assault, Bob looked up to see Emily Davis, who had approached noiselessly over the grass, standing over them.

'And what,' she said grimly, 'are you two doing?'

'Only looking,' quavered Bob, rubbing his ear.

'I call it *prying*,' said Emily. 'It's not only extremely rude, it could be very frightening to anyone inside the room. People's homes are private places. How dare you behave like that!'

Emily was very angry indeed. Looking back, Bob realised that she was anxious for her mother, as well as being affronted by such anti-social behaviour.

The two struggled penitently to their feet and apologised.

'Do you know what people like you are called? 'Peeping Toms', that's their name, and pretty mean they are reckoned to be. The police look out for 'Peeping Toms', so you'd better not do it again.'

The boys, thoroughly scared, promised fervently never to pry again.

'Then be off home with you. If I catch you at this again, there will be real trouble,' said Emily fiercely.

In silence, the two boys left the garden. In silence, they walked home along the muddy lane.

'See you Monday,' said Bob diffidently, when they reached the Picketts' gate. Ted grunted in reply.

Severely shaken, Bob Willet went on to his own home. It was the end, for him, of his secret game. Was it the end of his friendship, too, with Ted Pickett?

Mrs Willet was at the sink, washing up the tea things, when he entered. The table had been cleared.

'You're too late for your tea,' said his mother shortly. 'You should get home at the right time. You've been told often enough.'

She tossed him a tea-towel.

'Make yourself useful,' she said.

Dejected and hungry, wiping up the plates of those who had eaten, Bob Willet learnt his bitter lesson.

It didn't pay to be a Peeping Tom.

He never was again.

Mr Willet straightened his aching back and leant on his hoe.

Funny how fierce those little women can be when roused! Emily Davis could not have been much taller than he was, all those years ago, and yet the memory he had of her, on that distant evening, was of a vengeful giant.

Well, she'd put the fear of the Lord into him sure enough! It had been the right thing to do, no doubt, but what pleasure he'd had while the game lasted! Pity it had to end like that, but Emily was the very person to make a boy see sense. He might have scared the life out of some poor old soul one day. As it was, Bob's shameful secret was known only to Ted Pickett and Emily Davis. And they never told.

Mr Willet plucked a piece of groundsel from the earth and put it tidily with the heap of weeds.

'Good old Emily!' he said warmly, to the robin perched on the runner bean sticks, waiting for worms.

It would have made a fitting epitaph.

15 Off to America

IT was Mr Willet who passed on the news of Emily to Mr Lamb who kept the Post Office at Fairacre.

They were on their way to choir practice, prepared to tackle the usual Ancient and Modern hymns for the next Sunday, a fairly simple psalm, and a new anthem, which their choir-master Mr Annett, the Beech Green schoolmaster, called 'a refreshingly modern piece of music', and which the much-tried choir referred to privately as 'that hell-of-a-thing in E flat.'

'I'm sorry to hear it,' said Mr Lamb, entering the lych-gate. 'My brother George will be too. I'll mark the notice in *The Caxley Chronicle* when I send it on next week.'

'Does he find time to read the paper in New York?' asked Mr Willet, half-jokingly. George Lamb was known to be a prosperous restaurant owner there. His progress had been viewed with mingled admiration and envy by the Fairacre folk, but George's stock had risen considerably recently by his generous contribution to the repair of Fairacre's church roof. Those curmudgeonly souls like Mrs Pringle had been considerably sweeter in their attitude to George Lamb since that warm-hearted gesture of George's and his American friends.'

'He likes to keep in touch with things back home,' replied Mr Lamb. 'No friends like old friends, I always say. Emily

Davis was one of them, come to think of it, though we never saw a lot of her. George would be the first to say so.'

They crunched up the gravel path to the vestry door. The sound of the organ greeted their ears.

'Lord love old Ireland!' exclaimed Bob Willet, 'Annett's started already! We'll cop it.'

Like two naughty schoolboys, the two middle-aged men slunk shame-faced into the choir stalls, and Emily Davis was temporarily forgotten.

It was a cold blustery day when George Lamb opened *The Caxley Chronicle* faraway across the Atlantic.

'See P. 16' was written in his brother's handwriting on the top of the first page. He turned to page sixteen obediently, and read the brief notice of Emily Davis's death, marked by the pen of Fairacre's Post Office.

He lowered the paper to the counter, folded it carefully, and adjusted his coffee machine. His eyes strayed to the window. On the sidewalk the citizens of New York struggled against vicious wind and rain. In the shining road the traffic edged its way along, the windscreen wipers flicking impatiently.

But George saw nothing of the scene. He was back in time, back in Caxley, back in the Post Office living room at Fairacre, where his trip to the States had first begun, so long ago.

When George Lamb left Fairacre School at the age of fifteen, the Second World War had been over for almost two years.

Times were hard. Rationing of food was still in existence, and the basic necessities of life, houses, work, transport and even clothes were all in short supply.

Old Mrs Lamb still ruled at Fairacre Post Office, assisted by her older son. George, it was decided, should try for work at Septimus Howard's new restaurant in Caxley market-place. With any luck, he might be taught the bakery business too. There was a double chance there to learn two trades. One, or both, could provide George Lamb with a livelihood.

The boy cycled daily to work in all weathers, and thrived on it. At that time, Septimus Howard, respected tradesman and chapel-goer, was an old man, and within a year or two of his death. Mrs Lamb had a great regard for him, and was proud to think that George was in his care. Many a time she had listened to Sep's preaching, for she was a staunch chapel-goer herself, and Sep, as a lay-preacher often came to the tiny chapel at Fairacre to give an address.

'If you do as Mr Howard tells you, and follow his example,' she told young George, 'you won't go far wrong.'

She had been widowed whilst George was still a small boy, and sound instinct told her that a man of Sep's worth could be of untold value to the boy in his impressionable years. He certainly influenced George's thinking, and gave him an insight too, into the way of running an honest business.

It was Sep's idea that George should learn the bakery business first, and he began in the usual humble way of watching methods, weighing ingredients, checking the heat of the ovens, and so on, before proceeding to mixing and making himself. He was a conscientious lad, and Sep, always gentle with young people, took extra pains with the promising boy.

As time went on, he became skilled at decorating both iced cakes for the baker's shop and the enormous rich gateaux for which the restaurant was becoming famous.

He had his midday meal in the kitchen at the rear of the restaurant, with its view of the peaceful Cax through the window. This substantial meal was a great help to Mrs Lamb whilst food was still hard to come by. In the evening the boy ate bread and cheese, washed down with a mug of cocoa, with the rest of the family.

There were still contingents of United States troops stationed in the Caxley area. Howard's Restaurant was a favourite rendezvous for the men, and young George became friendly with several of them. One in particular, a blond young giant with a crew-cut, was a frequent visitor, and he and George struck up a friendship.

He was the son of a restaurant owner in New York. His father, so George gathered, was another Septimus Howard, hard-working, teetotal, and a stalwart of the local chapel. His son was inclined to be apologetic about his father's somewhat rigid views but it was plain to George that Wilbur was secretly very proud of the old man and of his business ability.

'You want to come and see the place for yourself sometime,' said Wilbur.

'No hope of that,' responded George. 'No money for one thing. And I've got a lot to learn here yet.'

'My old man expects me to go into the business.'

'Well, you will, won't you? Lucky to have something waiting for you.'

Wilbur looked thoughtful.

'I guess I don't take to the idea, somehow. Been brought up among pies and cookies all my life. I kind of want a change.'

'Such as?'

'Well, now you're going to laugh. I've a girl back home who works in a dress shop. I reckon the two of us could run a shop like that pretty good.'

'Have you got enough to set up a shop?'

'Nope. That's the snag. But if my old man could put up the cash, we'd make a go of it, never fear. It's just that he's looking to me to take over some of his jobs when I get home. It'll take a bit of breaking to him.'

'And you want me to take your place?' queried George jokingly.

'Well now, who knows? You keep it in mind, George. You might do a lot worse than try your luck in the States. Plenty of scope there for a chap like you.'

George did not give much thought to the conversation. His present mode of life was full enough, and besides he doubted if his mother would approve of a son going so far away.

Mrs Lamb was a strongly possessive woman, and hard times had made her calculating as well. With the wages of both John and George she managed fairly easily. She had an eye for a bargain, went shopping regularly in Caxley market on Thursday afternoons, and took advantage of every cheap line offered by the shops. The thought of losing either son's contribution to the housekeeping was a nightmare to her, although she was better off than many of her neighbours.

At that time, John was courting a local girl, and having considerable trouble with his mother on that account.

'I've nothing against her,' said Mrs Lamb, mendaciously.

'Except her being in existence at all,' thought John privately, but keeping quiet for the sake of peace.

'But can you afford to get married? Where are you going to live? She's welcome here, but I don't suppose this place is good enough for her.'

'It's not that, mother—'

'I'm quite prepared to take second place, hard though it is. I haven't had an easy time, as well you know. Bringing up two boys all alone, with mighty little money, is no joke. Not that one expects any thanks. Young people are all the same – take all, give nothing.'

This sort of talk nearly drove John Lamb mad at times. He saw quite clearly that self-martyrdom pleased his cantankerous old mother. He also saw the cunning behind it. As long as she could stave off the marriage, the better off financially she would be.

Things came to a head when his girl delivered an ultimatum. Her younger sister became engaged, and their wedding day was already fixed. This galvanised the older one into action. It was unthinkable that young Mary should steal a march on her!

'Well, do you or don't you?' demanded John's fianceé. 'If we have to live here for a bit, I don't mind putting up with your mum as long as we know we're getting a house of our own, in a few months, say. But if you can't leave your mother, then say so.'

'Don't talk like that,' pleaded poor John, seeing himself between the devil and the deep sea.

'I'm fed up with waiting. If you don't want me, there's another man who does. He's asked me often enough.'

'Who's that?' said John, turning red with fury.

'I'm not saying,' replied the girl, a trifle smugly. As it happened, John Lamb never did discover who the fellow was. Could he be mythical? John often wondered later on.

But the upshot was that John's wedding was arranged very quickly, and a double celebration took place in Caxley that autumn, much to the delight of the brides' father whose pocket benefited from 'killing two birds with one stone,' as he put it bluntly. As the poor fellow had four more daughters to see launched, one could sympathise with his jubilation.

The atmosphere in the Lamb household, between the time of the girl's ultimatum and the wedding, was unbearable. Old Mrs Lamb went about her Post Office duties with a long face, and had the greatest pleasure in confiding her doubts and fears to all her customers. Most of their sympathy went towards John and his wife-to-be.

'Miserable old devil!' was the general comment. 'I wouldn't be in that girl's shoes for a pension! If John Lamb's got any sense he'll clear out and let his old mum get on with it.'

It was at this unhappy stage that George began to think seriously of Wilbur's suggestion. He began to dread his return home, as he cycled back from Caxley each evening. Sometimes a brooding silence hung over the kitchen. Sometimes his mother was in full spate – a stream of self-pity flowing from her vigorously.

'How I shall manage I just don't know,' she complained one evening. 'It's bad enough keeping three of us going with what little comes in. When there's a fourth to feed, it'll come mighty hard.'

George's pent-up patience burst.

'Maybe there'll be only three after John gets married. I'm thinking of leaving Howard's.'

There was a shocked silence.

'Leaving Howard's?' shrieked his mother. 'What's this nonsense?'

'I'd like to go to the States. Got an opening there.'

This was not strictly true, but George was enjoying his mother's discomfiture.

'You'll do no such thing,' declared Mrs Lamb, recovering her usual matriarchal powers. 'You've got a good job with Mr Howard, and you're a fool to think of throwing it up.'

'I could do the same work in New York and get twice the money. Besides I want to see places. I don't want to stick in Fairacre all my life. If I don't go now, when I'm free, I'll never go. I'll be like old John here, married and stuck here for life.'

'And what's wrong with that?' demanded his mother. She looked at her younger son's rebellious face, and changed her tactics.

'And doesn't your poor mother mean anything to you?' she began, summoning ready tears. 'The sacrifices I've made, for you two boys, nobody knows. I've skimped and saved to feed and clothe you, and what do I get? Not a ha'p'orth of gratitude!'

She mopped her eyes.

'I only hope,' she went on, raising her eyes piously towards the ceiling, 'that you two never find *yourselves* unwanted by your family. A widow's lot is hard enough without her own flesh and blood turning against her!'

'Now, mother, please—' began soft-hearted John, who could always be moved by tears.

But George was made of tougher stuff.

'Any children of mine will have a chance to do as they want in life,' he told his mother stoutly. 'What's the sense in keeping them against their will? We all have to leave home sometime. I'm thinking about it now. That's all.'

'And what about the money?' said Mrs Lamb viciously.

George looked at her steadily.

'Let's face it, ma! That's all you're worried about.'

His mother turned away pettishly, but not before George saw that his shaft had struck home. He followed up his advantage.

'I'll get better opportunities in America. After a bit, when

I've got settled, I'll probably be able to send you a darn sight more each month than I give you now in a year.'

An avaricious gleam brightened his mother's eye. Nevertheless, she clung to her martyrdom.

'And how do we manage until you make your fortune?' she asked nastily.

'As other mothers do,' said George. 'I'm going to talk to Mr Howard. He'll understand how I feel. I shan't let him down, but I intend to go before long.'

Knowing herself beaten, Mrs Lamb rose to her feet, reeling very dramatically.

'I shall have to go and lie down. All this trouble's made my heart bad again.'

John took his mother's arm and helped her upstairs in silence.

Sitting below, at the kitchen table, George heard the bed springs creak under his mother's eleven stone.

John returned, looking anxious.

'D'you mean it?' he asked. 'Or are you playing up our mum?'

'I mean it all right,' replied George grimly.

As luck would have it, he came across Wilbur next day, and told him how things stood. Would he mind asking his father what the chances were for a young man in the trade?

Wilbur threw himself into George's plans with a whole-hearted zest which gave the boy encouragement when it was most needed. He was now quite determined to leave home. He would stay until John's marriage, but as soon as that was over he hoped to get away.

He did not intend to approach Sep Howard until he had heard from Wilbur's father. If he was discouraging he might just as well stay a little longer with Howard's, finding lodgings in Caxley. Whatever happened, he was not going to stop at home.

For one thing there would be little room for him when John married. For another thing, he foresaw that there would be trouble between the two women, and he was going to steer clear of that catastrophe.

But for all his determination, George suffered spells of doubt, particularly at night.

Lying sleepless in his narrow bed, he watched the fir tree outside the window, as he had done since he was a little boy. The stars behind it seemed to be caught in its dark branches, as it swayed gently, and reminded him of the Christmas tree, sparkling with tinsel, which he and John dressed every year. He would miss Fairacre, and his home. There would be no sparrows chirruping under the thatch, close to his bed-head, in

New York. There would be no scent of fresh earth, or the honking of the white swans as they flew to the waters of the Cax.

And was he treating his mother roughly? In the brave light of day, he knew that he was not guilty. At night, he became the prey of doubts.

There was, too, so much to consider. Suppose he hated America when he got there? Could he ever save enough for the return passage? He knew no one there – not a soul. Here he knew everyone, and they knew him, and his mother, and his forefathers.

And that, thought young George, thumping his pillow, was what was wrong! He felt stifled in this closed little world. He must get away to live, to breathe, to be – simply – George Lamb, a man on his own, not just a son, a grandson, a workmate or a neighbour – but someone in his own right!

The letter from Wilbur's father was lengthy and full of good sense. There were plenty of openings. He gave him a rough idea of wages to be expected, and the cost of living. He pointed out certain difficulties a country-bred boy might find in a foreign town, and prejudices which might have to be overcome..

On the second page he came to his proposition. In a few months' time his assistant was leaving to take over a new restaurant which Wilbur's father was opening. If George's references were completely satisfactory (this was underlined heavily), he would consider taking him on when the vacancy occurred. If, at the end of a month, either of them wanted to end the arrangement, well – fair enough. There were plenty of caterers in New York who would give a steady young man a chance.

Until he found suitable lodgings he was very welcome to stay with Wilbur's family. Any friend of Wilbur's – and so on.

George's spirits rose as he made a note of the address. He would write as soon as he had talked with Sep.

* * *

The frail old man listened attentively to the boy's tale. He had lived in Caxley all his life, and knew something of Mrs Lamb's possessiveness. He knew, too, that young George would prosper wherever he went. Rarely had he had such a promising pupil. He was a lad brought up on hard work, ambitious and adventurous and with a strong sense of justice. It was this last, Sep surmised, which had sparked off his revolt.

He advised the boy to talk of the matter, yet again, with his family. He told him that he would be able to give him excellent references, and he suggested that his own solicitor, Mr Lovejoy of Caxley Market Place, might find out more about the proposed job and his employer, so that the affair could be put on a business-like basis.

Within a month it was almost settled. If only his mother would bow to the inevitable, thought George! He would go so much more cheerfully if she gave the venture her blessing, but she continued to play the martyr.

It was at this stage that Dolly Clare and Emily Davis entered the scene. They had called together in the late afternoon to buy stamps. Dolly Clare, who had been button-holed many times to hear about Mrs Lamb's woes, hoped that they would escape this time, but it was not to be.

Emily Davis had not heard the tale first-hand, Mrs Lamb noted with satisfaction, arranging her face into the drooping lines of suffering widowhood.

'And so, off he goes, in a few weeks' time, whatever happens, I suppose,' continued Mrs Lamb lugubriously, after ten minutes' brisk narration of George's unfilial actions.

'They're all the same, Miss Davis, aren't they? No thought for their parents. Everything taken for granted. What happens to us old folk, don't matter. They must do as *they* want, no matter who's hurt by it'.

'You don't expect him to stay here all his life, do you?' said Emily, smiling.

'John will,' replied Mrs Lamb.

'Then you are very lucky,' responded Emily. Mrs Lamb began to look even more disgruntled than usual. It was a fine thing when your own generation turned on you!

'I wouldn't mind so much,' said Mrs Lamb, changing her ground, 'if he was going to someone we knew. But to be thrust among strangers! Well, it's hard for a mother's heart to bear, I can tell you. To think of my boy, alone and friendless in that wicked city—'

'No worse than London, I expect,' said Emily mildly. Mrs Lamb ignored the interruption.

'With all its temptations – and we all know what those are for a young man! No, I wouldn't say a word against this trip,' went on Mrs Lamb, waxing to her theme, 'if I thought there was anyone there he could turn to, if he was in trouble. Just one, just one single person! It's all I'd need to set my mind at rest.'

'That's easy,' said Emily. 'I've a brother in New York. I'll give you his address.'

She put down her handbag and reached for a pen and paper. Mrs Lamb's jaw dropped. Here was a blow!

At that moment, she heard the sound of George's bicycle

being lodged against the wall. The door burst open and there stood the young man, wind-blown and boisterous.

'I'm just telling your mother,' said Emily, still writing busily, 'that I hope you'll look up my brother in New York. He's a policeman there. Been there nearly twenty years. He's married with four children. He'd love to see you. This is his address.'

George held out his hand gratefully, and studied the slip.

'This isn't far from Wilbur's father's place from the look of it,' he said. 'I'm very grateful, Miss Davis.'

'Well,' said Emily, with a hint of mischief in her voice, 'your mother said she wouldn't mind you going one bit, if there were someone there you knew. So now you are settled.'

Mrs Lamb's face was a study in suppressed wrath. Her heavy breathing boded no good to George when the ladies had left, he knew well. He could have laughed aloud at the situation. This had taken the wind out of the old girl's sails all right!

'I'll write to my brother to tell him you are on your way,' promised Emily. 'How lucky that I called in! It must have been meant, mustn't it, Mrs Lamb? Good luck, George. I'm sure you're doing the right thing!'

Eyes sparkling, Emily Davis followed Dolly Clare through the door.

'Doing the right thing,' echoed Mrs Lamb, when the couple were out of earshot. 'That Emily Davis! Always was too fond of interfering in other people's business.'

'It pays off sometimes,' said George, tucking the address in his pocket-book.

He had such a grin on his face that for two pins his mother would have reached up and boxed his ears, but she forbore.

She would keep her recriminations for that meddlesome Emily Davis next time she saw her, the hussy!

'You look pleased with yourself,' said one of George's regular customers, offering a dollar bill. 'Had good news?'

'Not really. Heard of a death actually.'

'Gee, that's sad! Sorry I spoke.'

'That's all right. She was a very old lady – over eighty.'

'Don't suppose she's many friends left to mourn her then. Not at that age.'

'You'd be surprised,' said George, handing over the change. 'You'd be surprised! Emily Davis has got a lot in common with our John Brown.'

'Our John Brown?' echoed the man, puzzled.

'Sure. The chap whose body lies a-mouldering in his grave.'

'And whose soul goes marching on?'

'That's the lad. Emily Davis is right beside him, take my word for it.'

The customer nodded and made his way to the door. These English guys had the screwiest ideas, no matter how long they'd lived in a decent God-fearing country, he told himself.

16 Heatwave in London

THE day of Emily's funeral was quiet and grey. No breeze stirred the leaves or rustled the standing corn beyond the churchyard yew trees. Only a wren, hopping up and down the stairway of the hedge, added minute movement to the scene.

The church at Beech Green was small and shadowy. It was also deathly cold, despite the warmth outside. The congregation shivered as they waited for Emily to make her last journey up the aisle.

Dolly Clare sat in the front pew with several of Emily's nephews and nieces. Doctor Martin, who had attended both friends, sat behind her with Mr and Mrs Willet beside him.

Other Fairacre friends were nearby. There were relations and friends from Caxley, and a great many from Springbourne. But very few were Emily's contemporaries, for she had outlived the majority of them.

Among those from Springbourne was Daisy Warwick, whose husband was a bank manager in Caxley. She represented Springbourne Women's Institute, on this occasion, for she was the President of that branch. But she was also there on her own behalf, for she had been very fond of Emily Davis, and grateful to her for the care and affection she had shown to her only daughter Susan.

Daisy Warwick contemplated her well-polished shoes as she

waited, and wished she had put on a thicker coat to withstand the bone-chilling damp of the church. Her fore-arms, protruding from the three-quarter length sleeves of the sober grey coat which had seemed the most suitable garb in her wardrobe, were covered with gooseflesh, and her hands grew colder and colder inside her gloves.

This would not do any of them any good, she thought practically; particularly poor old Miss Clare, and the vicar, Mr Partridge, who served the parish of Beech Green as well as Fairacre, and had recently returned from hospital. At least he was warmer waiting outside for the coffin to arrive.

At that moment, the sound of the bier's wheels on gravel was heard, and the congregation rose as the voice of Gerald Partridge fluted the unforgettable words at the west door.

'I am the resurrection and the life, saith the Lord: he that believeth in me, though he were dead, yet shall he live: and whosoever liveth and believeth in me shall never die.'

Later that evening, Daisy Warwick made a note on the telephone pad in her hall. It was the last of several such notes. The page now read:

> 1 yard black petersham
> Buttons or zip?
> Mary's baby
> Lunching at Aunt Bess's on Sunday
> Cushions?
> Miss Davis dead.

For this was the evening when she made her weekly telephone call to Susan in London, and unless she had a list before her she found that the precious minutes had slipped by, and the things which she really wanted to tell the girl had been forgotten.

The weekly list was always a source of great hilarity to her husband whenever he waited by the telephone. There was something surrealistic about the juxtaposition of such items as: 'Uncle John's asthma cure' and 'Try really ripe Stilton', or 'Theatre tickets' and 'Bed socks'. The present week, with its jumble of dress-making, births, deaths, lunches and cushions, was well up to standard, and he commented upon it to his wife.

'Well,' she said truthfully, 'life's like that.'

And her husband was obliged to agree.

Susan Warwick shared a flat in Earls Court with four other girls. The rooms were large and lofty. The windows were the sash variety, of enormous size, and as the flat was on the first floor, it was light. This was one of its few advantages.

Susan shared a bedroom with Penny Way. The other three shared the second bedroom. The sitting-room, heated by an archaic gas-fire whose meter gulped down shillings at an alarming rate, overlooked the front garden. The kitchen and bathroom, both small and dismal, were huddled together on a landing at the back of the house half a floor below. It was hardly surprising that the girls lived mainly on toast, made over the gas fire, with various spreads upon it, or bowls of soup which could be heated easily on the kitchen gas stove and carried aloft to be drunk by the fire.

The house had been built in 1890 when three resident servants had been considered the absolute minimum for keeping such an establishment running properly. It was now owned by a gentleman who lived very comfortably in

Switzerland, and whose interest in this house, and a number of others which he owned, was purely financial.

Susan's house was now divided into four parts. The ground floor and basement were occupied by two young men, one with a sable coat and a pink rinse, the other with a black velvet cloak and a blue rinse, who minced off at eleven each morning and returned long after midnight, invariably squabbling at the top of their high-pitched voices.

On the floor above lived two young couples, and a newly-born baby who cried nightly, and wrung Susan's soft heart with its misery.

Up in the attics, where once the three maids had slept in more affluent days, lived a middle-aged artist who sometimes emerged with a portfolio of drawings, but more often sat in a haze of cigarette smoke, a bottle beside him, in his eyrie, and contemplated fame – preferably without working for it.

Of all the motley inhabitants, Susan found him the most repulsive. They occasionally met on the stairs. During the year in which she had lived there, she had watched him deteriorate from a slovenly, garrulous good-for-nothing into a shaking, morose wreck of a man. He had lost a great deal of weight, his eyes watered, his head trembled uncontrollably. His clothes, always stained and spotted, were now filthy and torn. Susan suspected, from the reek of the man, that he was now drinking methylated spirit. She flattened herself against the wall, and held her breath as he passed, praying that he would not engage in facetious conversation. She need not have worried. He now scarcely noticed her as he groped his way up and down the stairs.

After a year of London life under these conditions, Susan was beginning to have doubts. During her last year at school in Caxley, the thought of living in London in a flat, away from all who knew her in Springbourne, seemed the height of sophistication. Oh, to be free!

She was happy at home, and fond of her parents and brothers. The two boys were some years older than she was, and were already out in the world. Susan envied them, and was rather sorry for herself, left behind, over-duly cosseted, in her opinion, by her father and mother.

It was too much, she felt, to be obliged to be in by ten every night. And why on earth, she asked herself privately, should she tell her parents who she was with every time? Couldn't they trust her? Heaven knows, at seventeen she was old enough to look after herself!

Or was she? In her less rebellious moments, Susan admitted that her parents were only doing their duty. There were occasions when Susan had found herself non-plussed – even frightened. There had been that drunken youth at the bus-stop. Only Susan's speed and natural agility had kept her from his unwelcome embrace. Then there was that dubious party at Roger's where everything was plunged in semi-darkness and everyone seemed remarkably gloomy until mysterious tablets were passed round. Susan had had the sense to make her way to the bathroom, throw away her tablets, and creep from the house.

Her own home seemed doubly welcome after that incident. She lay in bed and looked with pleasure at all her much-loved treasures. There were her books, ranging from babyhood's Beatrix Potters to last week's purchase – a Penguin edition of a pop-singer's autobiography.

The bedside lamp cast a cosy amber glow over the patchwork quilt her mother had made. Normally, she considered it hideous and rather sentimental. Her mother was given to fingering sections here and there, saying: 'Isn't this sweet? Part of your first smock, darling.' Or, 'Grandma gave me this. It came from a tablecloth she bought in Lisbon.'

But after Roger's horrible party, even the patchwork quilt had its charm, and her parents, looking up from their books when she returned early, had seemed so sane and wholesome that she had kissed them heartily, much to their surprise and pleasure.

After she left school, she took a secretarial course in London, living in the hostel attached to it and going home thankfully most week-ends.

She found the work gruelling, particularly shorthand. On the other hand, the rudimentary French and German which she had already taken at school, was so slowly and so badly taught that she sat through each class becoming more and more furious. She tried, in vain, to get her parents to cancel these extras.

'Oh, I'm sure it will come in useful, dear,' they replied vaguely. 'Just do your best and be patient.'

'But it's wasting your money!' Susan persisted.

'Well, that's our loss, isn't it? We want you to make the best of your time there.'

The greatest attraction of the secretarial college was Penny Way. Penny had been at school with her, but a form ahead. She was an attractive girl, dark and lively, and outstandingly good at acting. To Susan, she had always been something of a heroine. At college, Penny was still one jump ahead, for she was living in the Earls Court flat whilst Susan was incarcerated in the hostel.

Penny was kind, in an off-hand way, to her junior and Susan

was suitably grateful for her condescension. Occasionally, they travelled back from Caxley to London on the Sunday evening train, but Susan was careful not to intrude if Penny happened to be accompanied by a young man.

In the last week of the last term, Susan obtained a post in an advertising agency in Kensington. She was talking about lodgings to a bevy of friends when Penny approached.

'We need another girl,' she said. 'Barbara's off to Geneva. Like to join us?'

Susan glowed with pleasure.

'Better come and see the dump,' said Penny, 'and meet the others. Then we can tell you about rent and so on, if you're interested. Come about eight. We usually eat at seven.'

If Susan thought this was rather cavalier treatment, the unworthy thought was instantly dismissed, and she presented herself at the shabby front door with its flaking paint, at eight o'clock promptly. No-one answered the bell, and she stood at the top of the flight of dirty steps, surveying her surroundings.

They were not inspiring. The minute front garden had two jaded variegated laurel bushes as its sole adornment. On the sour black earth, which did its best to nourish this natural growth, were cigarette cartons, sweet wrappings, a saucepan lid, several grimy plastic bags and a child's plastic beach shoe.

On the steps, leading from this square yard of flotsam to the young gentlemen's basement, stood a posse of unwashed milk bottles, a small red dustbin with no lid, and an extraordinary number of screwed-up bags which had contained potato crisps. Presumably, the occupants consumed these as their main item of diet, thought Susan.

Having rung the bell a second time, with no result, she

opened the door timidly. She was in an outer hall, once whitened daily with hearth-stone no doubt, but now grey and dusty. A door, with frosted glass in its upper half, led her into the main hall.

This, and the stairs leading from it, were covered in brown linoleum. Susan mounted the stairs, hardly conscious of the grime around her, so thrilled was she at the thought of emanicipation ahead.

It was very dark on the first floor, but the sound of music thumping away behind one door must mean that someone was home. She banged loudly upon it, and Penny flung it open, looking surprised.

'Oh, hello! I forgot you were coming. Come in.'

The noise from the ancient gramophone was deafening, and the fumes from the gas fire were equally stupefying. Two girls lolled, one at each end of the vast broken-down couch, their trousered legs lodged on the back of it. They did not move as Susan was brought forward.

'Barbara,' said Penny, giving no hint of which one she was. 'And Jane. Dobby's out, and Pam's doing her face. This is Susan.'

Barbara and Jane nodded in a friendly way, but said nothing. They seemed to be attending closely to the music, in a stunned sort of way. Susan was not surprised.

'Well, this is it,' said Penny, waving a hand vaguely to indicate the amenities of the room. Susan looked about her, observing the frayed and dirty curtains, the sagging armchairs, the greasy rug in front of the fire, and the two enormous oil paintings of Highland scenes which occupied most of the wall space. But her spirits rose. She could settle here very happily – particularly if Penny were here.

'Better see the bedroom,' said Penny, leading the way across the landing. 'This is ours.'

Two single beds were lost in the vastness of what had once been the main bedroom of the house. In the enormous bay window, in front of the sagging net curtains, brown with London dirt, stood a small dressing-table *circa* 1935, with plenty of chrome fittings and a badly-spotted looking-glass. Apart from two cane-bottomed chairs and a rickety chest of drawers with grained marmalade paint, this seemed to be the only piece of furniture in the room. Here again was the ubiquitous brown linoleum, but beside each bed lay a thin strip of carpeting which had once been a stair carpet, judging by the worn stripes across it.

'The beds aren't bad,' said Penny, giving one a thump. 'But you'd better bring your own sheets and blankets. Towels too, of course – and a few tea-towels would help.'

'I could do that,' said Susan, still besotted.

Penny went before her to the kitchen. If the rest of the accommodation had been disheartening, then this was downright repellent, and even Susan's spirits quailed. An enormous black frying-pan, full of congealed fat containing pieces of burnt onion, potato and bacon rinds, dominated the gas stove. This itself was an ancient monster, furred with the black grease of many years.

The walls of the kitchen ran with small rivulets of condensation which had left lines of brown encrustations over the years. A naked electric light bulb, covered with a fine film of grease, hung over the stove. The one window was tightly shut, and papered with an oiled paper representing stained glass. It was not very convincing.

'Window won't open,' commented Penny laconically, observing Susan's glances. 'All the windows have the jim-jams, but there's such a hell of a draught from most of them I think we get all the fresh air we need.'

Susan nodded half-heartedly.

'Next door's the loo,' went on Penny, throwing open the door of a dismal room housing a vast peeling bath, encased in pitch-pine, and a regal-looking lavatory seat with tarnished brass fittings. A snarl of tangled water pipes, flaking generously, wreathed about the walls and gurgled.

'How do you heat the water?' asked Susan.

'There's a boiler down below, and an old dear is supposed to keep it going. She comes every morning – in theory, that is. Mostly the water's tepid. We chuck in a kettleful of boiling water to pep it up, and get a decent bath when we go home.'

'What about rent?'

'We pay thirty quid a week.'

'What? Each?' shrieked Susan, appalled.

'Don't be funny. Six quid apiece. Can't get anything for much under. The gas fire's extra, of course. And our grub. We usually buy our own.'

'I think that will be all right. I'll have a word with my parents next week-end and tell you then. Is that all right?' asked Susan anxiously.

'Fine,' said Penny carelessly. 'Start the first of next month, if you want to come. Barbara's off then.'

She closed the bathroom door after three resounding bangings. At the third, the brass door knob came away in her hand. She thrust it back expertly.

'Better say farewell now. I'm due to go out in ten minutes and my current young man swears like a trooper if he's kept waiting.'

Susan said goodbye, and made her way downstairs and into the street. A small Negro girl, her frizzy hair sticking out in a dozen small plaits, each ending in a flighty scarlet bow, was busy jumping up and down the steps. She looked up at Susan, bright-eyed.

'You live there?' she queried.

'I'm going to,' replied Susan, smiling.

'I wouldn't,' said the child, still jumping.

Susan went on her way, elated by this exchange. Later, she was to wonder if it had not been some sort of warning.

Her parents had been very understanding about the flat, although Susan's mother was shocked when she saw it, by the conditions under which Susan was going to live, and she said so.

'It's nothing but a slum. Will you really be happy there?'

'Of course I will. Hundreds of other girls live in far worse places than this. It only wants a good clean.'

'It needs blowing up, and rebuilding,' said Daisy Warwick. 'But if you are prepared to live here, my dear, we'll do all we can to make you comfortable.'

Sheets, blankets, towels, a chair, some saucepans and crockery were carried from Springbourne to Earls Court. A large box of useful tinned food and some jars of home-made jam and marmalade, as well as bottles of fruit from the Warwicks' garden made their way into the rickety store cupboard in the flat's kitchen. Susan prepared to enjoy life.

On the whole, she was happy for the first few months, although there were several things about sharing which annoyed her. During the first week she spent Saturday afternoon washing the paintwork and scrubbing the floor of their bedroom. She cleaned the windows as far as she could reach, and polished the battered furniture. Even if the room did not look much more attractive, at least it smelt clean.

It was as much as she could do to remain silent when she saw Penny flicking cigarette ash to the floor that evening. She realised before many days passed that Penny was hopelessly untidy, and thought nothing of borrowing anything in the flat without bothering to ask permission. Scarves, jewellery, tights, even coats were missing when Susan looked for them, and her opinion of Penny, once so high, now plummeted.

It was annoying too to see how the groceries, which she brought to the flat, were eaten readily by all and not replaced. She did not mind putting in her share, nor doing her part of the sketchy daily cleaning and shopping, but it soon became apparent that she was carrying most of the burden. Hating to quarrel, she did her best, but resentment began to grow.

The advertising job did not work out as she hoped, and she left after three months and took a post with a typing agency. This meant that she was sent out to different offices which were short-handed. The pay was good, and she thought that the varied experience would be useful.

She found that the experiences were varied all right. One of her temporary employers turned out to be a dipsomaniac, two were addicted to stroking her legs, and another – a hard-faced woman journalist – had such a vitriolic tongue that she reduced Susan to tears within half a day. But on the whole, she enjoyed the work and gloried still in her independence.

She went home less and less, and when her parents did see her they began to grow increasingly anxious. Hurried meals, late nights, stuffy offices and the slummy flat were taking their toll. Susan had lost weight, had a series of painful boils, and was so tired that she spent most of the week-end asleep.

'Why don't you come home for a time,' urged her mother. 'You can always go back if you want to, but whatever's the good of earning these large wages if they all go on rent and fares? And just look at you – all eyes, and as thin as a rail!'

'Lovejoys need a secretary,' added her father. 'They'd be decent people to work for. And I met Mallet at Rotary lunch yesterday. He is looking for an assistant. There are plenty of openings locally. Do think about it. Your mother and I would love to have you at home.'

That had been in June, and very tempting Susan had found the offer. But she still clung to her independence. It would be a retrograde step, she felt, to return to Springbourne – almost an admission of failure. She turned her back on the garden, sweet with roses and strawberries, on the haymakers in the fields and all the joyous freshness of early summer, and went back to London.

It was harder to bear than ever in hot weather, and that summer was long and fine. The journeys across London by bus or tube were a nightmare in the rush hour. After a day at work, it was almost unendurable to squash among hundreds of other tube-travellers, all hot, perspiring, and as cross as she was herself. One evening of sultry heat, she fainted on her feet, but the crush was so great that she remained upright, supported by a kindly Jamaican giant who insisted on refreshing her from his hip flask, and poured most of it down her new cotton frock.

The flat was more squalid than ever. The windows refused to open, and the smell of stale cooking hung about the place revoltingly. By late summer, Susan was heartily sick of the whole sordid set-up. It was as much as she could do to speak civilly to the other girls. She was tired of having no privacy, no quietness – for the gramophone seemed to play endlessly – and no time in which to sit and rest, to mend her clothes, to read or to write letters.

On the day of Emily Davis's funeral, while her mother was shivering in Beech Green church, Susan was pounding her typewriter in an airless top-floor office. She sat immediately below a large sky-light, which would not open, and was hotter than she had been all the summer. She had elected to work through her lunch hour, as the letters upon which she was engaged were urgent. An apple and a glass of tepid water from the cloakroom tap were all that she had eaten during the day, and by the time she arrived at Earls Court station she was almost too tired to walk to the flat.

Everywhere seemed filthy. A hot breeze raised the dust, swirling pieces of paper across the pavements. Dogs lay panting in the scanty shade of porches. Children in bathing suits lolled on the steps of houses, too hot to play. Men, stripped to the waist, sat at open windows, their arms dangling across the sills, to catch what little air there was. Querulous babies cried in stuffy prams, turning their wet heads this way and that to try to ease their wretchedness.

The traffic rumbled and roared continuously, like some snarling monster. To sit in a moving vehicle was misery on a day like this. To sit in a stationary one, in a traffic jam, was more than human flesh and blood could endure. The blaring of horns added to the din.

Susan stripped, and had a tepid bath, then lay, exhausted, upon her bed. She must have fallen asleep for the telephone bell roused her. Bemused, she struggled from her bed to the sitting-room. For once, it was mercifully empty.

Her mother's voice sounded reassuringly near.

'And how are you?'

'Terribly hot.'

'Here too, dear. Thunder, I think. Mrs Smith is getting on with the suit and says will you get a yard of black petersham for the skirt top, and do you want a zip or buttons?'

'Buttons. I'll get them.'

'Right. Now the next thing. Mary Bell is having a baby at Christmas. Isn't that nice?'

Susan forbore to say that Mary had told her this some time before, so early, in fact, that Susan had felt it was tempting fate to mention it.

'And Aunt Bessie's asked us to lunch on Sunday, so bring a frock, dear. You know how she feels about trousers.'

'If it's as hot as this, I'll probably go nude.'

'Yes, well – I thought I'd let you know. And do you still want those two cushions? If not, they can go to the Scouts' jumble sale.'

'Can I tell you at the week-end?'

'Of course. And the last thing. I've been to a funeral this afternoon at Beech Green. Now, *there's* a place to get cool! That church is like an ice-well.'

'Anyone I know?'

'Miss Davis. Your old teacher at Springbourne.'

'I'm sorry. Poor old dear – but I thought she'd died years ago. She must have been a hundred.'

'Eighty-something, I believe. She'll be missed. She was always so kind.'

'She was indeed,' agreed Susan. The pips sounded peremptorily.

'Well, we'll see you on Friday night, dear. At the station. Goodbye.'

'Goodbye,' said Susan, putting the sticky receiver back in its cradle.

She must make a note about the petersham and buttons, and get them tomorrow in her lunch break. And the cushions? She looked about her, at the depressing airless room, and the broken couch which, she thought, the cushions might make more bearable.

To hell with the cushions! Why should she bother to make the place look decent! No one else did. She'd fought a losing battle long enough. She wished she need never set eyes on the dreary place again.

She went to the window and tried for the hundredth time to open it. A sash cord broke under her onslaught, but the window remained firmly closed, sealed tightly by the paint.

Panic seized her. She could have smashed the grimy glass at that moment, in her frantic longing for air. Oh, to be on the downs at Springbourne, to feel the wind lifting one's hair, or to feel the cold rushing breeze as the swing flew up and down from the beech tree in the garden. If you swung high enough, you could see over the hedge to the village school across the way.

The village school! And Miss Davis! Susan rested her hot forehead against the grimy window pane, and stared unseeingly at the traffic pounding below.

Miles and miles away. Years and years away. And now Miss Davis was dead. A different world – a quiet, happy world of light and air and sunshine – or so it seemed, thought Susan, looking back.

17 Snowdrops at Springbourne

SUSAN had known Miss Davis and the village school for as long as she could remember. The Warwicks had moved to Springbourne when Dudley Warwick was appointed to be manager of the Caxley branch of his bank, a few years after the war.

The house was a comfortable and solid building, put up between the wars. The first owner had made a fine garden, and the Warwicks, who were keen gardeners themselves, were glad to find mature trees and hedges, settled pathways and well-tended flower beds, when they took over.

Susan was born at Springbourne, and her earliest memories were of her afternoon outings in the pram. The school was less than a quarter of a mile away, and the children were usually setting off for their homes, after school, when Mrs Warwick and Susan returned from their walks.

Miss Davis was often at the gate, seeing off the children safely, and always had a word with Mrs Warwick and the child. Emily's hair was greying by this time, but her eyes were as dark and sparkling as ever they were. They reminded Susan of the bright glassy eyes of her much-loved toy monkey. There was a humorous twinkling look about them both, which the child found irresistible.

At five years old she went to the school herself. It was the autumn term, and the beech tree in the garden was already beginning to drop leaves as bright as new pennies.

She was happy from the first day, for several of her friends were there, and she knew that home was only a short distance away.

As so often happens, the newcomer picked up measles as soon as it appeared in the village. She had it more severely than most, and Doctor Martin insisted that she stay at home for the rest of the term.

'It's not a thing to take lightly,' he told Mrs Warwick, who privately thought that the old man was making a mountain out of a molehill. 'It goes in cycles. At the present time, it's very severe. We don't want complications. She can go out, well-wrapped up as soon as she is out of quarantine, but I don't want to risk any further infection.'

Susan chafed at the delay in returning to school, but revelled in the short walks she took with her mother when she had recovered.

She loved to collect flowers and stones, or any other lovely treasure which she came across in the hedges or fields. In those few weeks was born the deep love of natural things which was to stay with her for the rest of her days.

When she returned to school after the Christmas holidays she seemed perfectly fit, but Mrs Warwick noticed that she still tired easily if she took too much exercise. Miss Davis promised to keep an eye on the child.

One morning in February, Miss Davis came into the infants' room and told them that they were going to have a treat.

Mrs Allen, the farmer's wife, who was also one of the school managers, had invited them to her garden to see the snowdrops. They grew in vast drifts in a small copse at the edge of the garden, and thicker still in a dell near the house which had once been a sawyer's pit, many years earlier. The garden was famed in the Caxley area for its profusion of snowdrops, and the children were excited at the thought of an outing to such a lovely place.

There was much bustling in the school lobby as the young children buttoned coats and wrapped scarves round their necks. The infants' teacher was left in charge of Miss Davis's class, while the headmistress shepherded her little flock through the village to the farm.

It was almost a mile distant, but the sun shone and their spirits were high. A thick frost still sparkled on the grass verges and the bare twigs, but some golden catkins told of spring at hand, and a blackbird sang from a thornbush as boisterously as if it were April.

Mothers at their dusting waved and called to them as they passed, and tradesmen gave them a friendly toot on their horns as they went by. Altogether, it was a glorious occasion, made even more splendid by the knowledge that normally they would have been closeted in the schoolroom.

Susan skipped along with the others joyfully, but was glad when the farm gates came in sight, for her legs had begun to ache. Miss Davis, noticing, offered to carry her, but Susan would have none of it. However, she held Miss Davis's warmly-gloved hand, and was secretly glad of this support.

The snowdrops were so unbelievably white and pure, so numerous and so far spread, that the children fell silent in wonderment for a moment. Susan thought how like snow they were – not only in their whiteness, but also in texture. There was something crystalline in the drooping heads, delicate and opaque in the morning sunlight. The greyish-green spears of leaves set off the purity of the flowers perfectly. It was an unforgettable sight.

They were allowed, by kind Mrs Allen, to wander about freely and to pick a small bunch each. What is lovelier than picking flowers, especially when they are the first after so many dark months of winter? The earth was moist and fragrant beneath the trees, and here and there the tiny leaves of the honeysuckle showed the first brave touches of spring.

When they had had their fill of these joys, the children walked back along the drive to the farm kitchen. On the way Mrs Allen picked ivy leaves to put with each bunch. Susan thought the dark glossy leaves, mottled like marble, were a perfect contrast to the white beauty of the snowdrops. Every year, she promised herself, she would have just such a February nosegay to remind her of this wonderful morning.

Beyond the back garden of the farm, a row of calves pressed against the low hedge. Their shaggy heads hung over it inquisitively. Their beautiful eyes, heavily fringed, gazed solemnly at the children, who gazed back just as solemnly.

The ground fell away gently into the distance, and then rose again to the swelling flanks of the downs, scarcely visible in the morning haze. To Susan, the distance seemed vast. She was suddenly conscious, for the first time, of the infinity of space about her, as she stood on the little hill in the shelter of the farmhouse.

The calves' breath floated up like steam, in the forefront of this picture, from their shiny wet noses. Far away, the farm dog must have seen the children, and began to race down the slope of the distant hill towards them.

At first he was a dim black shape moving swiftly towards his home, but as he drew nearer Susan thrilled to the sight of his splendid movement as he stretched his legs as rhythmically and as proudly as a racehourse. His ears flapped, his white teeth were bared in a grin of ecstasy, and when he finally reached them, he was so warm and panting, so full of vigorous life and spirits that Susan felt her own strength and excitement rising at the sheer joy of being alive on this tingling day of early spring.

They went into the great farm kitchen, after much shoe-wiping supervised by Miss Davis.

There on the table stood two steaming jugs of milk and an array of mugs and glasses. There was also a yellow china bowl filled with ginger biscuits.

As she sipped her milk among her chattering companions, Susan was conscious of the sudden contrast between this warm room, full of colour and conversation, and the great empty airiness outside. Both were lovely, one in its cosy domesticity, the other in its limitless mystery.

Her physical tiredness made the child more sensitive to her surroundings than usual, and she suddenly became aware that, for her, she must always have both worlds – each was necessary and complementary. One was her nest. The other was the place in which she stretched her wings, and soared, as effortlessly as the lark outside, into a different dimension.

When elevenses were over, and the mugs had been put into the sink, and the beautiful ginger biscuits had all been eaten, the children thanked Mrs Allen individually and shook hands with her, as Miss Davis had told them to do earlier. When it came to Susan's turn she felt that such formality could only express part of her feelings. She put her arms round Mrs Allen's ample waist and gave her a loving hug, when the official handshake was over.

By the time the little crocodile had reached the end of the farm drive, Susan's legs refused to carry her further, and she looked up at Miss Davis in despair.

'My legs ache,' she began, but did not need to add any more, for Miss Davis swung her up on to a high bank and sat down in front of her.

'A piggy-back for you, Susan. Up you get!'

The child gratefully put her arms round Emily's neck. Her teacher's dark wiry hair tickled Susan's face, but this was pleasurable.

She enjoyed jogging along, her cheek against Miss Davis's scarlet coat. Below her the children bobbed along, their bunches of snowdrops clasped carefully in their gloved hands. Their breath rose in silver clouds, as they clattered along in their sturdy country boots, and reminded Susan of the adorable calves standing against the background of mistily distant hills.

There was something wonderfully reassuring and comforting about Miss Davis's small strong body which bore her along so steadily. Emily had given many a piggy-back to younger brothers and sisters, as well as her own pupils, and had the knack of carrying a child in a way which gave most comfort to them both.

Susan never forgot that welcome ride. The experiences of that shining morning culminated in the new bond forged between teacher and pupil as they made their way together through the village.

Standing listlessly at the stubbornly-shut window of the flat, Susan noticed once again the small Negro girl sitting on the kerb opposite.

She was clad in a grubby elasticised white bathing suit. Her bare feet were thrust into a pair of silver evening sandals which might have been her mother's, so large were they. She rose to her feet lithely, and began to teeter along in the grotesque shoes, looking, for all the world, Susan thought, like Minnie Mouse.

Suddenly her amusement changed to pity. There she was, poor child, about the same age as she had been on that far morning of sparkling light and infinite airiness, but doomed to spend the day in a noisy prison of stone and brick. It was all wrong! No child should be forced to endure this claustrophobic squalor!

For that matter, no one – child or adult – should have to endure such conditions.

The memory of the snowdrops, the memory of Miss Davis, the memory of the calves and the emptiness beyond their endearing heads, flooded back to Susan. Why not go back?

She knew in her heart that these two worlds still existed side by side – the small and the limitless. Too long she had suffered from being penned. It was time to find her true self again, and for that she must have space and air and beauty.

It could be done. She could give in her notice tomorrow, telephone to her mother and ask if she could come for a week or two's holiday. She knew how joyously she would be welcomed. Who knows? She might find that job in Caxley after all.

But that was in the distance. All that mattered immediately was to escape – to put her affairs in order, in this swarming filthy ant-hill she had once thought so glamorous, and to find quietness and space for the survival of her body and mind.

Perhaps that had been the secret of Miss Davis's strength, she thought suddenly. She went at her own pace, and had time to relish all the lovely natural things in Springbourne and thereabouts. And when the occasion arose, that happiness, fed by inner serenity, could succour the weak and give, as Susan could so poignantly recall, strength and heart to those who needed it.

She went into the bedroom and began to pack in readiness for a longer stay at home than usual. She was not going to make up her mind one way or the other. No doubt London would pull her back before long, just as Springbourne tugged her now with an urgency her starved spirit must obey.

But she would go forward with her immediate plans. Her spirits rose as she moved about her work in the sultry heat. Soon she would be out on the windy hills above Springbourne, where the small happy ghost of Emily Davis had beckoned her.

Her mind raced ahead. She saw herself at the booking office in the deafening and dirty London terminus. Aloud, she rehearsed the words:

'Single to Caxley!'

18 Doctor Martin's Morning Surgery

A WEEK or two after Emily's funeral, Doctor Martin sat in his surgery at Beech Green, awaiting the first of the day's patients.

The morning was warm and rather close for October, and the windows looking on to his garden were wide open. A bed of mixed roses stood immediately below the windows, and in the quietness the doctor could hear a blackbird busily scrabbling the earth for worms. Now and again a delicious whiff of the roses' scent wafted into the room, giving the old man much pleasure. His love of roses grew greater as the years passed.

He glanced at the silver clock on the mantelpiece. Nine-thirty. Time he opened shop, he told himself.

He smoothed his grey hair and opened the door into the little waiting room. Not many today, thank heaven. Fine weather cut his queue by half. It was in January and February that extra chairs had to be put in the waiting room.

'Good morning! Good morning!' said Doctor Martin cheerfully.

'Good morning,' replied his sufferers, with varying degrees of joy.

Doctor Martin consulted his list.

'Mrs Petty?'

A stout young woman rose, carrying a toddler, and followed Doctor Martin into the surgery. She was, in fact, Miss Petty, but the birth of Gloria, who now accompanied her, accounted for the change to a married title.

The Pettys were a large family, originating in Caxley. They ran to fat, were short-necked and inclined to respiratory diseases. They were also good-tempered, happy-go-lucky and quite incapable of keeping to any diet prescribed by their various doctors for weight reduction.

'Well now, what's the trouble?' asked the doctor kindly.

It appeared that Gloria's 'summer cold' refused to go. She complained of a sore throat, and had a stubborn cough which grew worse at night.

'Let's have a look,' said Doctor Martin, fishing the spatula from a glass of disinfectant.

Gloria began to wail.

'Give over, do!' begged her mother. 'And open your mouth.'

Doctor Martin expertly held down the child's tongue during one of the lulls in her whimpering.

'Tastes nasty!' whined the child when the instrument was removed.

'Maybe,' said the doctor amiably. 'I should think most things taste nasty with that throat.'

He pressed her neck glands, and then took out his stethoscope. After the examination, he sat at his desk and wrote the prescriptions.

'Now, this one is for tablets which she must suck slowly. Not more than six a day, mind you. Read the label carefully. You can read, Mrs Petty?'

The question was asked casually. There were still several people among Doctor Martin's patients who were unable to read despite a century of compulsory education.

'A bit,' replied Mrs Petty

'Not more than six during the twenty-four hours. They should settle the infection.'

He held up the second slip of paper.

'This is the cough cure recipe. A teaspoonful when it is troublesome.'

She took the two papers almost reverently, and put them carefully inside a dilapidated patent leather handbag. She was about to leave when Doctor Martin motioned her to the chair again.

'This child's tonsils want attention. Bring her back in a fortnight. And her teeth have caries – are going bad. That means the second ones may be infected. She's having too many sweets, Mrs Petty. Cut them out.'

'But she likes a bit of chocolate! Her gran brings her a bar every day!'

'Ask her to bring an apple instead. Chocolate will rot her teeth and make her too fat. She's overweight now. You're storing up trouble for the future, if you don't feed her properly. We've talked about this before.'

'Well, I'll try,' said Mrs Petty grudgingly, 'but it's her gran you ought to talk to.'

'Are you still working?' asked the doctor, showing her to the door.

'Every afternoon,' said the woman, her eyes brightening. 'Down the new fish shop. It pays for me bingo, Mondays.'

'D'you take the child too?'

'No, Gran comes up. I leaves a bit of tea for 'em both.'

Doctor Martin had seen those teas once or twice. Bought pies, packets of crisps, sliced wrapped bread, glutinous shop jam and a pot of well-stewed tea. Not a ha'p'orth of nourishment in the lot! Even the milk was tinned. He had seen the opened tin standing on the table, with a large blow-fly in attendance.

'See the child gets eggs, fresh milk, some meat and plenty of fruit,' said Doctor Martin for the hundredth time. 'She needs building up.'

He opened the door, and Mrs Petty made her departure.

'Building up,' she echoed, when she gained the lane. 'He's gettin' past it. Says the kid's too fat and then, in the next breath, wants buildin' up.'

'Can I have an ice-cream?' cried the child, as the village shop came in sight. 'Can I, mum? Can I?'

'I'll see. Doctor only said: "No sweets." Yes, all right. I'll get you a lolly, love.'

She felt quite sure an ice-cream wouldn't hurt her. After all, mothers always knew best.

* * *

Doctor Martin worked his way steadily down the list of patients. There were a few unexpected visitors among them, such as Joe Melly the shepherd, who had nicked the top off a troublesome spot on his wrist, and who now had a fat shiny hand which throbbed painfully, and a dangerous red line creeping up his arm.

There was seventeen-year-old Dicky Potts, with yet another boil to be lanced. There was garrulous Mrs Twist, who enjoyed fainting fits when life became too much for her – or she was getting the worst of an argument. Jane Austen would have diagnosed the vapours. Doctor Martin could do little more. There were the two youngest children of Minnie Pringle, smothered in spots, hot, flushed and tearful, with furred tongues and high temperatures, who were despatched to bed promptly by the old doctor.

'And I'll call in on my rounds,' he told scatter-brained Minnie, who stood looking more like a bewildered hen than ever. 'They've got measles. You should have had more sense than to bring them out, Minnie.'

Might as well talk to a brick wall, he told himself, watching the trio depart up the lane.

'Who's next?' he asked of the two or three remaining patients. Mrs Barber, a comparative newcomer to Beech Green, rose with her daughter, a fair-haired schoolgirl, and the two followed Doctor Martin into his surgery.

'What's the trouble?' asked Doctor Martin of the mother. She gazed at him in silence and, to his dismay, her mouth began to tremble and her eyes fill with tears.

The doctor turned to the girl who was looking at her mother with mingled impatience and disgust.

'Are you the patient?'

'I s'pose so,' the girl shrugged.

Mrs Barber produced a handkerchief and blew her nose noisily.

'We think she's in trouble,' she said tremulously. There was only one condition which was described to Doctor Martin in these terms.

'Then I'd better ask you a few questions,' said the old man gently.

He put them simply, and the girl replied in an off-hand way. Obviously, the mother was more upset than the daughter.

'Lie on the couch,' directed Doctor Martin, 'and we'll have an examination. There's nothing to fear.'

When it was over, and the suspicions confirmed, the doctor told them that the baby would be born early in March, and gave them the address of the ante-natal clinic. He was kind and uncensorious, doing his best, by being completely matter-of-fact, to ease the tension of the unhappy situation.

'Perhaps you would wait outside a moment, while your mother has a word with me,' he said.

When the girl had departed, the mother's tears began to flow again.

'The shame of it! Only sixteen – barely seventeen when the baby comes – and no father! What will the neighbours think? We've given her everything she wants, tried to bring her up nice, and now look what's happened!'

Doctor Martin let her run on in this vein until she had had her outburst.

'Did you explain the facts of life to the child?'

'Well, no. It's so embarrassing, isn't it? You know, it never seems the right moment. Anyway, the school should teach her that these days.'

'These days,' said the doctor, 'are much the same as any other days. Parents still have duties towards their children.'

'I blame her Gran,' said Mrs Barber, sniffing. 'She was supposed to go there straight after school on the days I was working. She never bothered if Audrey was late. I bet all this happened then.'

'And how old is her grandmother?' asked Doctor Martin mildly.

'Eighty – but very healthy.'

Doctor Martin felt some sympathy with this absent and elderly scape-goat, and said so.

'It's no good casting round for someone to blame,' he

continued. 'You know the situation – it's all too common, unfortunately – and you must all make the best of it as a family.'

'That boy'll have to marry her,' said Mrs Barber fiercely.

'If he loves her, he'll want to,' agreed the doctor, 'but I can't see anyone benefiting from a shot-gun wedding, least of all your daughter and the baby.'

He patted the woman on the shoulder, and walked with her to the door.

'Say as little as you can to her until you've had time to cool down. You'll say things you'll regret all your life if you are too hasty now. Look after that girl of yours. She needs all the help she can get, silly child, and you're the one she'll turn to, if you'll let her.'

He watched the two depart, and beckoned his last patient into the surgery.

Elaine Burton was fifty-two, as Doctor Martin knew well, but she might have been sixty-two from her haggard looks. Her husband worked at a printer's in Caxley and her two children also worked there. They were unmarried and still lived at home.

Mrs Burton's main problem was her old mother, now nearly ninety, who lived with them. Brought up in a strict Victorian way, the old lady remained a martinet despite failing health. Her daughter, acting as buffer between the demands of the younger generation and the old, came off worst in the household, as Doctor Martin knew well.

'I think I need a tonic,' said his patient wearily. 'I'm tired all day, and when I get to bed I can't sleep. Mother needs seeing to at least twice in the night, and I think I've got into the habit of being on the alert all night. It's really getting me down, Doctor Martin.'

He surveyed the woman with an expert eye. She had been pretty once. He remembered her as a young woman with her first baby. She had been trim and lively, with soft dark hair, and a quick smile which revealed dimples.

Now she was running to fat, and was pale and listless. Blue smudges under her eyes bore testimony to lack of sleep. Her hair was lank, her neck decidedly grubby. Her whole bearing spoke of exhaustion and self-neglect.

'I'll put you on some iron tablets,' said the doctor, drawing his pad towards him. It was plain that the woman was anaemic and over-worked.

'How's your appetite?'

'I don't fancy much. By the time I've spooned mother's food into her, I don't want my own.'

'Do you have a cooked meal?'

'When the others get home, but I don't really want it then.'

'Milk? Eggs?'

'I could never take them, even as a child.'

The old doctor sighed. Here was yet another case of the dying sapping the living, but what could one do?

'And how is your mother?'

'To be honest, a terrible trial, doctor.'

'Can't your brother have her for a while? To give you a break?'

Mrs Burton snorted.

'He's under his Ethel's thumb, and she refuses point-blank to give any help with ma. Besides, ma hates her like poison. It would never do.'

She could have added that her own husband's attitude was much the same as Ethel's, but loyalty kept her silent.

'We might be able to get the old lady into a home, you know.'

'She'd never hear of it. And I wouldn't want to send her away, despite all the work. It's the washing and drying that gets me down. I have to wash bedding and nightgowns every day – sometimes twice a day. It's far worse than having a baby to look after. Still, it's got to be done. I wouldn't have her moved. She's my mother, after all.'

'Do the young ones help?'

Elaine Burton gave a hard laugh.

'They take the tray up now and again, and switch on the radio for her, but that's about the lot. They nag me to send her away, and she nags me to keep them quiet, and tells me I've not brought them up respectful. You know how it is.'

Doctor Martin nodded sympathetically. He knew indeed.

He felt sorry for them all – the unhappy, cross old lady, confined to her bed; the exuberant young people criticised at every turn, the husband condemned to watch his wife's health slowly seeping away and, chiefly, Elaine Burton torn this way and that, by the demands of all, and fast becoming too tired to carry the heavy burden of the combined duties of daughter, wife and mother.

'You should get away with your husband for a holiday,' he told her seriously. 'If your brother won't have your mother, I can arrange for her to go into hospital for a fortnight. Now, talk it over. I know it won't be easy, but it's no good knocking yourself up. Where will the family be, if you have to give up?'

The woman was visibly moved and gave him a shaky smile, as she held out her hand for the prescription.

'I'll think about it, but I can't see it coming off,' she said honestly.

Doctor Martin showed her to the door.

'I'll drop in and see the old lady one day soon,' he promised. 'Meanwhile, take those tablets, and some good food.'

He watched her go sadly, then returned for his bag. Off to see two of his patients in Caxley Cottage Hospital, and then he must set about his rounds, he told himself.

He locked his desk, and the drugs cupboard, and went thoughtfully to his car.

19 Doctor Martin Looks Back

CAXLEY Cottage Hospital was a small building erected in the twenties, and opened by the Mayor of the day with considerable civic pomp.

It served the area well, but now there were rumours of its closure, much to the indignation of the local people. As they pointed out to each other, by the time you had been dragged all the way to the county hospital, twenty miles distant, and waited in the queues of traffic which had to be encountered on the way, you would probably be dead on admission.

'And who wants to go all that distance to visit relatives?' they demanded. 'And who can afford the fares there, anyway? A dam' silly idea shutting the Cottage. Hope it never happens.'

Doctor Martin agreed with them. He could quite see that a more modern operating theatre was necessary, and that the place was uneconomic to run, but there was still plenty of minor surgery and certain illnesses which could be dealt with in this little place, thus relieving pressure on the larger hospitals at the neighbouring towns.

His first patient was in high spirits when he went to see her in the children's ward. Mary Wood was seven years old, and had had her tonsils removed.

'Mummy's fetching me tomorrow,' she told him triumphantly. 'And I'm going to be home for tea. And I'm going to have a puppy.'

'What? For tea?'

The child smiled indulgently at this little joke, revealing a gap where her two front milk teeth had vanished.

'I'm not a *cannibal*,' she answered, bringing out this new, half-understood word with considerable pride.

The remark amused Doctor Martin for the rest of the day.

His other hospital patient was less cheerful. Old George Smith was recovering from acute bronchitis, and was fearful of what the future might hold.

'My old woman ain't up to nursing me, sir, and we can't abear the idea of living with our Nell, good girl though she be. They've got them two strapping boys, hollering about all day, and playing that electric guitar all night fit to blow yer 'ead off. Us old folks couldn't stand it, and they don't want us anyway.'

'Would she be able to look in to your home and give a hand? The district nurse could call each morning. We'll fix up something, never fear.'

'We likes to be independent,' said the old man obstinately. 'And anyway, our Nell goes out cleaning every morning; she's got enough to do. No, let's face it, doctor, you keeps us old folks alive too long these days – and we're not wanted. Time was, this bronchitis of mine would've carried me off. Now I'm still 'ere, and a nuisance to everybody.'

Tears of self-pity rose to his eyes.

'Rubbish!' said Doctor Martin robustly, patting the wrinkled hand on the coverlet. 'You're just a little low in spirits. Wait till you're home again! You'll be as fit as ever.

'If there's one thing I 'ates,' continued the old man, 'it's the work-house. I knows things is better now, but I can recall the time when 'usbands and wives were parted at the gate, and sometimes never saw each other no more. 'Twas a terrible thing that – to be treated worse than animals.'

'Things like that don't happen now,' the doctor assured him, but the old man rambled on, unconscious of interruptions.

'Seems to me the young people ain't got no respect for their parents today. They do say that in China the old folks are looked up to because they're reckoned to be the wisest of the family. Don't see much o' that in these parts. It's time I was dead, doctor, and that's the truth of it.'

Doctor Martin did his best to speak comfortingly to the old man, but it was clear that he was sunk too deeply in his own miseries and fears to heed much that was said.

Doctor Martin returned to his car and drove carefully through Caxley High Street. It was with a sigh of relief that he turned the nose of the car northwest, and regained the leafy lanes leading to Beech Green, Springbourne and Fairacre.

'Thank God,' he said aloud, 'my practice is in the country.'

He pulled off the road, as he so often did, on the brow of a hill. Here there was a fine view of the countryside, backed by the splendid whale-back of the downs.

The doctor wound down the window and breathed in the fresh air, tugging a pipe from his pocket as he did so.

He filled it, meditating upon his morning's work, and the people with whom it had brought him in contact.

What problems people had! If one believed all one read in newspapers and magazines, or saw at the theatre or on the ubiquitous "Box", the only problem besetting people these days was sex. Good grief, thought the doctor impatiently, that was a pretty minor problem, taking all ages of men and women into account! He'd put the problems of health, family and money, as being quite as important as sex – certainly from the age of forty-odd onward, which included a goodly proportion of the nation, after all.

His mind dwelt on poor old George Smith's worries. Here was the age-old difficulty of keeping the older generation happy and cared-for. Something had gone amiss with the pattern of family life today, making this problem even greater than it had been in earlier generations.

Yes, George had a point about being kept alive too long – but a doctor's first duty was to his patient, and he must do his best to prolong life. Nevertheless, it created problems for all.

He looked back upon his own memories. His grandmother had lived in a tall town house, four storeys high, and two unmarried daughters and an unmarried son lived with her. She had borne twelve children and eight had survived. The house always seemed full of nieces and nephews, of all ages, coming and going, bearing little presents, chattering about their families, showing Grandma their new babies, or pirouetting before the old matriarch as they displayed the latest fashions. There was a lot said against those large Victorian families, but at least there was a feeling of belonging – and even if there were battles now and again, a common enemy had only to appear to weld the clan into solid unity.

And then, there was always someone with time to spare. His maiden aunts seemed to be able to drop whatever they were doing to play shops with him. When Grandma's sight began to fail, one or other read out the items of news from the daily paper with real kindliness, it seemed to the child. No one seemed cross, or in a hurry, or resented serving the old lady, although no doubt there were times when they found her as tiresome as George Smith's grandchildren and poor Elaine Burton found their ancient relatives.

Of course, the burden had always fallen hardest on the unmarried daughters, and still did, for that matter. And then, so much depended on the old people's attitude to life. If they could keep busy, and avoid self-pity, it was half the battle against depression.

His grandmother, he remembered, always made herself responsible for the midday meal. She spent the morning preparing it, and the rest of the day planning for the next day's menu. She did little else in the house, but this one important chore eased the strain for everyone and, above all, gave her the inestimable reward of knowing she was useful.

He took out a match, struck it, and drew his pipe into life. Through the blue clouds, he gazed at the view spread out below him. The spire of Beech Green church pierced the surrounding trees, and his thoughts turned to his last visit there, when Emily Davis had been buried.

Now, there was a family which had managed its life well, he mused! When he first met them all, most of Mrs Davis's family were out in the world, and Emily went out to her teaching at Springbourne each day, but returned at night.

Every Sunday there seemed to be a family reunion. Sons and daughters from Caxley brought over their children for Sunday tea, and news was exchanged. They were a lively collection, Doctor Martin recalled, and there was plenty of laughter in the tiny cottage.

Perhaps that was the secret of happy family life – or one of the secrets. Nowadays people didn't seem to have time to laugh. All too busy rushing from place to place, like scalded cats, mused the old doctor, stirring the tobacco in his pipe bowl with a match-stick.

The Davises travelled very little. Poverty had its rewards sometimes. If one had to remain in the same place, then one made one's pleasures there. Certainly the Davis family created their own delights. They gardened, and saw the results of their labours in the fine string of onions hanging in the shed, the sack of home-grown potatoes, the jams and jellies ranged upon the kitchen shelf. They knitted and they sewed. Doctor Martin remembered the beautiful dolls' clothes which Mrs Davis made each Christmas for her granddaughters' presents. He had admired tucks and feather-stitching on the minute petticoats – work which no modern parent would bother to do – but which would be prized by the owner of the lucky doll, and give pleasure too to the needlewoman.

The little cottage overflowed with the results of their handiwork. The walls were papered by one son, the paintwork done by another. Rugs, cushions, chair-covers, all were made at home, and most of their clothes, too, were hand-made. It was a way of life which had endured for centuries, but which was now fast vanishing.

Doctor Martin recalled one of his favourite characters who had lived in the eighteenth century and kept a diary. Parson James Woodforde, although a fellow of New College, Oxford, did things with his own hands just as the Davises did. He brewed his own beer, he salted pigs, he kept his house to rights, he pruned and dug in his garden, as well as visiting his parishioners and serving the church. He had a great deal in common with the country folk of Doctor Martin's earlier memories, and his sense of family duty was as keen. He was concerned about Brother Jack, the black sheep of the family, and considerate to his niece Nancy who lived with him.

The latest over-worked word 'involved' came into the old doctor's mind. Those earlier people really were involved. Emily Davis, a good daughter, cared for her mother until her death, and did it cheerfully, just as she did her duty towards the many school children who passed through her hands.

She had been a wonderful person – perhaps the finest character in that fine family. One did not meet many quite as selfless these days. That perhaps was one of the causes of Emily's strength.

She was completely devoid of self-pity, unlike poor Elaine Burton and George Smith.

She shouldered responsibility bravely, unlike Mrs Barber who thought that the school alone should tell her daughter the facts of life.

She had an unswerving sense of justice, based on her Victorian upbringing of recognising right from wrong. It may have been too rigid a code, but it produced some good steadfast people who engendered those old-fashioned virtues of respect and duty.

Doctor Martin looked at the clock on the dashboard. It was time he moved on. His pipe was almost finished, and he had day-dreamed long enough. He must blame Emily Davis for much of it!

He wished he could tell her so. She would have enjoyed the joke. She always did.

He switched on the engine and drove gently down the hill to Beech Green.

20 Two Old Friends

As Doctor Martin slowly descended the steep, winding hill, he caught a glimpse of the tall figure of Dolly Clare moving about in her garden. On impulse, he drew into the side of the lane, and made his way up the garden path.

Miss Clare was cutting a few late roses, and she held them up for the doctor to admire.

'For Emily's grave,' she told him. 'Now that all those lovely funeral flowers have gone, it is beginning to look rather bare.'

The doctor nodded. He approved of the way in which Dolly

Clare talked so lovingly, and yet so calmly, of her dead friend.

'Mr Willet is going to plant a low bush of red roses for me on the grave. There won't be a headstone. Emily always set her face against any sort of permanent memorial.'

'She left her own memorial,' commented the doctor, 'she'll never be forgotten.'

Dolly smiled at him.

'Come inside. I've something for you.'

She led the way into the little cottage. It was as fresh and shining as ever. A vase of flowers stood on the polished table. The curtains stirred gently in the breeze from the open window. There was a delicious smell of something baking in the kitchen. It was quite apparent that Dolly Clare, old and bereft though she was, was still self-reliant, and still revelling in her independence.

'Do sit down,' she said, 'while I put these in water. I shall go up to the churchyard this afternoon, after my rest.'

He did as he was told and looked about him. It was obvious that Dolly was busy sorting out Emily's effects, for a large suitcase, propped open, was filled with clothes, and on the little bureau by the window were some trinkets which the doctor recognised as Emily's.

Dolly Clare returned with the roses in a vase and put them on the window sill.

'Coffee?' she asked.

The doctor shook his head.

'Not for me, Dolly. I'm getting up an appetite for lunch. It's curried lamb today, I'm told.'

Dolly laughed, and crossed to the bureau.

'As you see, I'm sorting out Emily's things, and I've practically finished. The nieces and nephews were remembered, of course, but she asked me, several times, to give you this as a little remembrance of her.'

She brought over to him a silver pocket-watch on a silver chain.

'It was given to her brother when he retired. He left it to Emily, and she always kept it on the little table by her bed. It's an excellent time-keeper. She hoped you would find a use for it.'

The old doctor was too moved to speak for a moment, as he turned the beautiful thing in his hands.

'How generous of her,' he said at last. 'I shall always treasure it, Dolly. Always.'

He undid his jacket and patted his waistcoat.

'Help me to put it on now, Dolly. It's going to be my constant companion.'

Miss Clare helped him to thread the chain through a button-hole, and the doctor put the watch very gently into his pocket. He stood up and surveyed himself in the mirror on the wall.

'Do you know, Dolly, I've always wanted a pocket watch, and never felt that I could indulge myself. This is doubly welcome – a remembrance of dear Emily, though she would be remembered well enough without it, as you know – and something I've always longed for.'

Miss Clare smiled.

'It would have pleased Emily so much to know you like it,' she told him. She turned to the bureau and held up a gold locket for the doctor to see.

'I wish I had found this earlier,' she said seriously. 'I should have put it in the coffin with her.'

She handed it to the doctor. It contained the portrait of a young man in uniform. He studied it for some moments, then looked questioningly at Dolly.

'Edgar,' she nodded. 'The only man she ever loved. Sometimes we used to say we'd both been unlucky in love. After all, we both lost our lovers – but we were wonderfully blest with all the affection we had from the children at school and all the friends about us here. It helped a lot, you know.'

'You both deserved happiness,' exclaimed the doctor.

Miss Clare sat down in the armchair by the fire.

'I was so touched by the dozens of letters I had. Some from as far afield as India and Australia – mostly from old pupils who had read the news in *The Caxley Chronicle* or in letters from home. And then there were a great many from people I scarcely knew – Jane Bentley, for instance, who taught with Emily many years ago, and Daisy Warwick. She wrote so kindly about Emily's care of her daughter.

'And the flowers, as you know, were unbelievably lovely. I'd no idea that Emily was so widely known. Even Mrs Pringle sent a beautiful heart made of Michaelmas daisies.'

'Well, that really is a tribute to Emily,' agreed Doctor Martin, laughing.

'And so many little kindnesses to me too,' went on Dolly. 'Mr Willet brought me a marrow – which I can't look at, incidentally, without remembering Manny Back, and Emily at her most mischievous. And I've been given enough fresh eggs by kind neighbours to keep me in omelettes for weeks.'

'I'm glad to hear it,' said the doctor. 'Mind you eat them, and look after yourself.'

He rose, and looked down at his new watch-chain proudly.

'I can't tell you how much I appreciate this,' he said soberly.

'This is a typical gesture of Emily's, generous and practical. I shall wear it always.'

He turned at the door.

'I'll call again, Dolly. Don't get over-tired. What are you doing for the rest of the day?'

'Finishing my sorting. I'm thoroughly enjoying looking through the old school photographs. I've recognised several Pringles and Billy Dove, and a host of others.

'Then I shall take the roses up to Emily's grave, and also plant a clump of snowdrops which I've dug up from this garden. Emily always loved them, and I went with her several times to see them at Mrs Allen's farm. What a glorious sight! Emily used to reckon it was one of the high-lights of the winter.'

'You're going to be busy I can see,' commented Doctor Martin. 'Well, better to wear out than rust out, as my old grandmother used to say.'

He waved goodbye, and Miss Clare watched him drive along the lane into the distance.

That evening, as dusk was falling, Dolly Clare took her accustomed walk at the edge of Hundred Acre Field, behind her home.

All her little duties were done, and she felt free to enjoy the evening air before settling by the fireside.

She reached the oak tree, and stood very still, watching three fine pheasants searching for acorns at the foot of the gnarled old trunk.

Above her the rooks were flying homeward. The great field before her, gleaming with gold when last she walked there with Emily, was now freshly ploughed, the furrows dark and glistening. Within a few days the seed would be planted and she would watch, alone now, the first tender blades appear, then the ripening crop and, finally, its harvesting.

The comforting cycle of the seasons continued unchanged – the sowing, the growing and the reaping.

Dolly Clare turned, and made her way homeward with a grateful heart. Life went on, and was still sweet.

Recommended Reading

Ali, Tariq, *Bush in Babylon: The Recolonisation of Iraq*

Al Rasheed, Madawi, *The History of Saudi Arabia*

Clarke, Duncan, *The Battle for Barrels: Peak oil myths & world oil futures*

Deffeyes, Kenneth S., *Beyond Oil: The view from Hubbert's Peak*

Goodstein, David, *Out of Gas: The End of the Age of Oil*

Heinberg, Richard, *The Party's Over: Oil, war and the fate of industrial societies*

Ismael, Jacqueline S., *Kuwait: Dependency and Class in a Rentier State*

Ismael, Tareq Y. and Jacqueline S., *The Gulf War and the New World Order: International relations of the Middle East*

Keay, John, *Sowing the Wind: The Mismanagement of the Middle East 1900–1960*

Klare, Michael, *Blood and Oil: How America's thirst for petrol is killing us*

Kleveman, Lutz, *The New Great Game: Blood and oil in central Asia*

Leggett, Jeremy, *Half Gone: Oil, gas, hot air and the global energy crisis*

Lewis, Bernard, *The Middle East: A brief history of the last 2,000 years*

Mobbs, Paul, *Energy Beyond Oil*

Phillips, Kevin, *American Theocracy: The peril and politics of radical religion, oil, and borrowed money in the 21st century*

Roberts, Paul, *The End of Oil: On the edge of a perilous new world*

Ruppert, Michael C., *Crossing the Rubicon: The decline of the American Empire and the end of the age of oil*

Simmons, Matthew R., *Twilight in the Desert: The coming Saudi oil shock and the world economy*

Tertzakian, Peter, *A Thousand Barrels a Second: The coming oil break point and the challenges facing an energy dependent world*

Unger, Craig, *House of Bush, House of Saud: The secret relationship between the world's two most powerful dynasties*

Vidal, Gore, *Dreaming War: Blood for oil and the Cheney–Bush junta*

Yapp, M. E., *The Near East since the First World War: A history to 1995*

Yates, Douglas A., *The Rentier State in Africa: Oil rent dependency and neo-colonialism in the Republic of Gabon*